NEW DAWN

A Tropical Coast Thriller - Book 1

RILEY CURTS

ISBN 978-1-7771515-4-6 (paperback)/978-1-7771515-5-3 (large print)/ 978-1-7771515-6-0 (mobi)/978-1-7771515-7-7 (epub)

NEW DAWN

PROLOGUE

THE MAN IN THE BROWN BASEBALL CAP MOVED ACROSS THE weathered boards of the dock like a shadow. Beside the hull of the boat berthed in the last slip, he stole a glance over his shoulder toward the shore behind him. Satisfied there was no one and he remained unseen, he let out a slow breath. Raw energy coursed through him and he rolled his weight onto the balls of his sneakered feet.

A sliver of gray light from the new moon fell across his face. The beak of his cap kept most of his features in darkness, except for the slight smile that tugged at his lips, marred by a jagged scar.

Reaching his arm to his back, he drew a dagger, the blade glinting softly in the weak moonlight, and pulled himself up onto the deck of the Papa Joe.

CHAPTER ONE

DAWN DEVON, CLAD IN HER USUAL CARGO SHORTS AND weathered black T-shirt, stood on the bow of the Papa Joe, sweating under the hot mid-day sun. She coiled the bow line while surveying her neighbor three slips down on the other side of the pier.

He was hopping mad. Literally hopping from his left foot to his right, dancing the dance of the deranged on the stern of his boat. All morning his curses had rung loud through the air as he threw wrenches and hissy fits, and repeatedly turned the ignition on the little engine that couldn't. Or wouldn't, apparently. Dawn was amazed he hadn't burnt out the ignition switch by now. Perhaps he had.

He glanced over in her direction and she quickly lowered her gaze and turned her head, not wanting to bear witness to his meltdown or be drawn into his drama.

Too late.

"Dawn," he called out.

"Ugh," Dawn said under her breath, wondering if she could ignore him.

Timothy Tyler Talbert, also known as Triple T behind his

back, hadn't been a favorite of Joe Black's—Dawn's mentor and the Papa Joe's previous owner. Over the last few weeks, Dawn had come to understand why.

His permanently rumpled clothing was rarely laundered, diesel oil clung to the creases of his knuckles and caked under his chipped and unkempt nails, his greasy hair clung to his head in clumps, and up close the air quality suffered tremendously, his sour breath and yellowed teeth testament to his two-pack-a-day habit.

He also smoked copious amounts of pot, claiming it as a medical necessity to help with his PTSD. The clouds of sweet smoke hung over the dock in the humidity like a London fog. In the evenings, the secondhand smoke alone could have Dawn reaching for the Doritos. She'd taken to keeping the cabin windows closed, a torturous decision in the sweltering Florida nights, but the fear of anything mind-altering tortured her more.

She turned her head as Timothy landed with a thump on the dock and called her name again. He stomped down the dock, his grimy fingers leaving an inky trail across his forehead as he wiped at the beads of sweat collected there.

"Got some WD-40?" He peered up at her, hand shielding his eyes against the sun. "I ran out." As usual, his abrasiveness and lack of greeting rubbed her the wrong way.

"I should have some below." Dawn dropped the line to the deck hoping to get to her tool chest and get him back on his way as soon as possible. Opening the hatch, she lowered herself into the forward cabin. Unfortunately, being out of sight was not enough.

"I've had a hell of a morning," Timothy grunted. "Hell of a morning."

Dawn had quickly learned it was best not to engage him. The smallest bit of encouragement could set him off for ten or twenty minutes. Life was too short.

Below, Dawn swiped a stack of marina bills, stamped Overdue in bright red, off a shelf and pulled out a small tool chest. Digging through it, her eyes strayed over to the plank below the starboard porthole where Joe had stashed the automatic rifle an hour before he died. It had nested there since. She wondered what the penalty would be for taking the rifle out, scooting back on deck, and blasting a big hole in Timothy's chest.

Tempting as it sounded, she turned her attention back to her tools and grabbed a can of WD-40.

"Yeah," Timothy continued, "I spent the whole damn morning trying to get that engine to turn over. I'm stumped. At this point, I have no freaking idea what the problem is."

"Sorry I can't help with that," Dawn said, popping her head up through the hatch. "I barely know my way around this engine."

"Yeaaaaah." Timothy stretched the word out, peering up into her eyes. "I figured," he said. "No offense, it's just, well, I know Joe was still teaching you the ropes. I mean, unless you already have some knowledge of engines, especially diesels, well..." His voice trailed off and he toed at a loose board in the pier.

Dawn could feel things getting out of hand. The last thing she wanted was to have to explain herself to Triple T. As far as she was concerned, the less he knew about her the better. "I found that WD-40 for you." She tossed the can down toward his outstretched arm and he caught it easily. Holding it in his hand, like he'd never seen a can of lubricant before, he tilted his head and read the label.

"Thanks," he said. "I'll give it one more shot. If I can't get it going, I'll have to call the mechanic out. Dammit. I can't really afford that right now."

Dawn stared down at him, uncertain how to get him to

move along. She levered herself back onto the deck. "Hope it works for you."

Ignoring her subtle hint, he asked, "You know who could've fixed this?" His bushy brows crawled up his forehead like wayward pollen. "Joe."

Dawn's chest tightened. She was shocked to see Timothy's features crumple before he dropped his chin to his chest to hide his face.

"I miss the old bastard, you know." His voice trembled.

The tightness in her chest inched up into her throat, and she swallowed. Hard. In spite of herself, she felt a softening toward him. They hadn't spoken about Joe's death since the funeral. Most of the guys on the dock, after the first week or so, had been awkward around her, not knowing what to say she supposed, and she'd been left to grieve alone. Not a horrible thing, because it avoided overly sentimental moments like this one that left her feeling uncomfortable. But the genuine loss in Timothy's voice touched her.

"I miss him too," she said.

"Yeah, well." He avoided her eyes as he turned away, waving the can in the air. "Thanks." He ambled off to his boat without glancing back in her direction.

Dawn sucked in damp air through her nostrils, held it in her chest, replacing the pain with oxygen, counted to ten, and breathed it out slowly.

Then she returned to the only thing that had kept her sane the last few weeks.

She got back to work.

··

CHAPTER TWO

··

Perched on a small stool on the dock, Dawn wielded the scraper against the hull of the boat where Felix, that asshole Cuban she held partly responsible for Joe's death, had not only scraped into the paint with his speedboat, but had also left a healthy gouge in the wood. Flecks of blue paint fluttered onto her knees and dusted the weathered boards beneath her feet, each fleck fanning the flame of her anger.

She'd done some reading about grief. The whole five stages thing. She was bouncing somewhere between denial, anger and bargaining like a broken pinball machine. People kept trying to tell her how to grieve and that pissed her off. People kept asking her for money and that brought out whatever bargaining power she had left. The rest of the time she lived in denial, as if by refusing to believe Joe was gone he would automagically appear one afternoon on the dock and chew her out for stowing something in the wrong place. Or push that silly cap back off his head, to scratch at his scalp while he took a minute to think.

Damn Timothy. Work had kept her busy enough until he'd come along looking for the WD-40. She refocused on the task at hand, forcing the morose thoughts from her mind.

The sun had tracked to the west, and she was shielded from the worst of its heat by the galley cabin. Working quietly in the shade, with only the sound of the water lapping against the hull, her mind drifted.

She'd been living on the boat for almost two months now. Not surprisingly, her landlord had kicked her out. Unable to come up with the rent, despite the threats and eviction notices he'd tacked to her door, she'd simply packed the few things she still owned and moved it all down to the boat a few days after Joe's funeral. She was sure he wouldn't have minded, and with nowhere to go and no one else to turn to, there wasn't a lot else she could do.

Even in death Joe had looked out for her, bequeathing her the Papa Joe to her and providing a roof over her head. But as the weeks had passed, the weight of wondering how she was going to pay the moorage fees had grown heavier. They were much higher than she'd imagined.

Initially, given the circumstances, the marina store manager had given her slack on the due date. But yesterday, after her daily workout in the member's gym, he'd called her aside and told her he was getting pressure from above to secure her payment and needed something from her by the end of the week.

What did that even mean, pressure from above? People with better offices on the top floor, not stuffed away in the basement near the lockers and showers and storage? Some higher power? God? A marionette master?

Regardless, the message had been clear. She needed to pay up. Sooner than later. The threat of being out on the street again was causing her to lose sleep. Not that her demons let her sleep that well anyway.

CHAPTER THREE

Earlier in the week, spurred on by desperation, Dawn had passed by her old gym. For almost two hours, she sat in the diner across the street, leaning against the familiar orange vinyl in a booth, staring out the window, building her courage. It'd been years since she'd been back. When the waitress had cleared away the dishes, stopped filling her coffee cup, and pointedly slapped a bill on the battered Formica table while lifting a carefully drawn-on brow, Dawn rose and made her way to the black door of the converted warehouse.

Squat narrow windows designed for natural light but long grimed beyond usefulness, lined the high walls a foot below the roof. Heart pounding against her chest, she turned the knob and stepped through the door into the murky shadows of the large, open space. A cacophony of sounds assaulted her. The slap of leather against leather, the grunts of men, the shuffle of quick feet against the floor, the muted encouragement of coaches and sparring partners.

The sharp smell of fresh perspiration laid over a lingering, vintage layer of old sweat was as familiar to her as warm apple pie. And almost as comforting.

Nobody had paid attention to the opening and closing of the door. Standing in the shadow of the wall, her eyes scanned the room. Mostly new guys but she recognized a handful of regulars from before. In the corners, near the punching bags and speed balls, a couple of coaches she didn't know worked with newer boxers, demonstrating technique and either encouraging, cajoling or berating depending on their style.

She took it all in before her gaze settled on the open office door in the far wall. Dust motes danced in the weak light that slanted out onto the weathered floor. Taking a step forward, she halted as a large man stepped into the doorway, throwing a long shadow across the stained linoleum. With the light behind him, she couldn't see his face, but there was no mistaking the form. She took another step forward. His head swiveled in her direction and he stepped away from the doorway, closing the distance between them with long, confident strides.

"As I live and breathe," Charlie said. His teeth flashed as he grinned widely.

Dawn forced her feet forward, stomach clenched, and extended her arm. Her hand trembled, and she forced a smile to her lips.

Charlie's eyes narrowed as he looked at her outstretched hand. Ignoring it, he stepped up to her, almost nose to nose, and enveloped her in a strong hug. "Jaysus, it's good to see you girl."

Overwhelmed, Dawn brought her arms up to Charlie's back. Once, he'd meant as much to her as Joe. Her eyes itched as they dampened. "I figured you'd forgotten me by now." She choked out the words, cursing her runaway emotions.

"You?" Charlie stepped back, his own eyes glistening, and stared down at her. "Don't imagine that would ever happen." He shook his large head, drinking her in, and she noticed the gray at his temples, the deepened creases near his eyes. "Not in a million years."

"Or a million tears," Dawn said, completing their old catch phrase.

"Anyway, you were always my favorite female boxer."

Dawn laughed. "I was your only female boxer."

He looped an arm over her shoulder and guided her across the floor. "Come have a cup of rot gut and catch me up."

As they worked their way back to his office, several of the men cast sidelong glances their way, curious about the young woman Charlie seemed so cozy with. He tipped his chin to a couple here and there, and Dawn nodded back to one of the men she recognized leaning against the ropes of the second sparring ring.

Entering Charlie's office was like stepping into a time warp. Old boxing posters hung from the wall, corners curled and torn from the silver thumb tacks fixed to the yellowed drywall. He used to talk about painting the walls, but operating funds were always tight, and there was never anything extra for anything so unimportant as cosmetic fixes.

The old water stain in the corner remained. The brownish discoloration wiggled down from the ceiling in a crooked line and then puddled into the shape of a boot. It had always reminded Dawn of map of Italy. There'd been days in Charlie's office, tuning out his ranting about one thing or another she'd done wrong, that she'd focused on that boot and dreamed of running away to Italy, living somewhere on the Mediterranean, eating fresh fish and Kalamata olives and rich feta cheese, and boxing only on weekends for recreation. Maybe she'd become a coach herself. Spend the week fishing in a colorful little skiff with an olive farmer with snapping black eyes.

Behind the cheap, serviceable desk, books and papers casually strewn on narrow shelves threatened to tumble to the floor. Piles of bills and envelopes and newspapers hid the surface of the desk. Charlie folded himself into the weathered leather chair. It creaked in protest at his weight as he rolled it across the small space to the coffee pot.

"Still take it black?" He motioned Dawn toward one of the wooden chairs.

She settled into the orange maple one on the right, always her preference, and reached forward for the chipped mug he held out to her. "Yes, thanks."

"So," Charlie said, stirring a heaping spoonful of sugar into his Daytona 500 cup, "catch me up."

Setting her coffee down, Dawn filled him in about the last few years, careful to skip over the less complimentary aspects of her life. By the time her untouched coffee was turning warm on the corner of the desk, she'd covered the highlights.

"I was sorry to hear about your brother," Charlie said.

"Thanks." Coming from Charlie, it meant something. Her lower lip trembled.

"And now you're living on a boat." Charlie pushed his chair back to the coffee pot and held it up in question. She shook her head while he topped his cup up. "I wouldn't have seen that coming."

"Honestly, that would make two of us." Needing to move the conversation in the right direction, she said, "Bring me up to speed on things here?"

Charlie's lips pursed, an expression she knew well. He was thinking of a way to break bad news. In this business, sometimes it seemed like bad news was the only news.

CHAPTER FOUR

After giving Dawn a snapshot of the last few years at the gym and his most promising fighters--who never developed into anything--Charlie put his coffee cup down, leaned forward with his elbows on the desk and fixed her in the beam of his warm brown eyes. "Jordy left me."

"What? For a better job?" For as long as she could remember, Jordy had been Charlie's right-hand man and the second most requested coach within a hundred miles of Merritt.

"Hung up his gloves. Threw in the towel. Gave up the ghost." He shook his head, his forehead furrowed. "I never thought I'd live to see it. His sister from up north retired to a place near Clearwater and offered Jordy the guest cottage to live in."

"That doesn't sound like Jordy. Sitting around doing nothing, I mean."

"He claims to like the pace. Says it's more relaxed than here." Charlie's lips tilted in a smile. "You won't be shocked to know he's already doing some part-time coaching. Started a boxing club at the local high school."

Dawn chuckled. "I wish I'd seen him before he left."

"He was always fond of you," Charlie said, his voice low. "We all were."

Unable to meet his eye, Dawn took a sip of cold coffee.

"Actually, I'm glad you came in." Charlie sounded more like himself and she looked up, a bit surprised. "With Jordy gone and summer coming, I'm short staffed. You'd make a great coach."

The words hung in the air, tangible as the May heat. It was exactly what she'd been hoping to hear. She took a deep breath. "How many hours would you need?" As much as she needed the work, she still had things to do around the boat.

"As many as you can spare. You know this place, there's always someone who needs help. We're running the same hours, and of course we have the after-hour keeners." He winked at her and she remembered the nights she'd spent alone in the dim corners with the speed ball.

"I might be a little rusty." The idea of stepping back in a ring made her insides quiver. Fear, sure, but for the first time for as long as she could remember, a small ripple of excitement coursed through her. All the hours she'd spent in the marina gym working out to avoid her grief might pay off in other ways. "You should know I broke my wrist a couple months ago. My lower body is the strongest its ever been though."

"Damn," Charlie said, his eye flicking to her left hand as she held it up. "How's it healing?"

Dawn shrugged. "It's coming. The cast has been off a couple of weeks. Doc says I need to go easy on it for a while."

"You won't be throwing any punches," Charlie said. "These kids would be lucky to train under someone like you. You might have been away, but you'll never be forgotten. Not in these parts."

"Hey Chuck." Charlie's gaze moved above her shoulder and Dawn turned to look at the young kid in the doorway. Solidly built, his cheeks flushed pink when he met Dawn's eyes before quickly looking back to Charlie. "You gonna have time for me today?"

"You betcha," he said, waving the kid away. "Twenty minutes on the speed ball to warm up."

The kid's eyes shot toward Dawn. "Hey, I recognize you. You're Tropical Storm Dawn." Her jaw dropped and the kid shrugged. "There's still posters of you in the back."

"I don't go by that anymore," Dawn said, struggling to keep her tone even.

"Get out of here," Charlie yelled. The kid backed away and Charlie put his palms up in the air. "See? Like always. Busy. So what do you think? Like I said, these kids need someone like you." Bracing his hands on the desk, he pushed himself up. Dawn couldn't be sure this time if the creaks came from the chair or his knees. Charlie wasn't getting any younger.

She stood as he came around the side of the desk. She had to ask. She didn't want to, but she needed to be able to lay out some kind of payment plan for the marina. "I'd love to. What kind of pay is involved?"

Her hopes fell as a shadow worked its way across Charlie's squashed features.

"Oh, shit," he stammered, "you know this place, Dawn. There's no money. It'd be... I don't know. Think of it as community service. A way to give a little something back, I guess."

Dawn's face heated and she swallowed. She'd love to have the time to give something back, and he was right, she owed him that much. She opened her mouth, then closed it again. But with the marina hot on her heels and the prospect of being homeless for the second time in as many months, she abandoned the last scraps of her pride. "Is there anything you could pay me for? Sweeping floors? Keeping the books?" she blurted.

Charlie sized her up and she could almost read the thoughts that flitted across his face. Like he should have seen this coming. Like she wouldn't willingly come back here only to catch up, or to offer a helping hand. That was unkind and harsh and fortunately Charlie had more compassion than she gave him credit for. He dropped a large paw on her shoulder. "You in a fix?"

CHAPTER FIVE

WAS SHE IN A FIX? DAWN'S GAZE FLICKED ABOUT CHARLIE'S office, to the water stain, the stack of bills on the desk, the worn equipment visible through the office doorway, the gaggle of ragtag kids, so reminiscent of herself at that age, eager for someone to coach them. Charlie had enough of his own problems.

She extended her hand. "It's all good," she said. "I should be on my way. You've got some coaching to do."

She backed out of the office, forcing a smile. "Once I get the boat up to speed, I'll come volunteer a few hours."

"You're welcome anytime." He walked back across the floor with her.

As the silence between them grew heavy, Dawn said, "Thanks for the coffee."

"Well, now I know you're desperate." He chuckled and waved her off as someone called his name.

Dawn shook her head, the brutal heat of the day grounding her back on the dock. As she pushed the scraper over the last of the chipped blue paint on the hull, the bitter taste of the coffee and defeat settled on her tongue again. She tossed the scraper into her bucket and went aboard to seek a cold drink.

———

Dawn popped the top of the cola and took a long swallow. Gulls circled overhead at the mouth of the harbor where a fishing charter headed back in. The ocean lay still as a bird bath. The echo of footsteps caught her attention, and she stepped to the port door. A young, wiry man lugging a large tool chest strode down the dock in her direction. Stopping at Timothy's slip, he yelled out a hello. Timothy had apparently given up on the little engine that couldn't and called in a pro.

She drained the soda, dropped the can into the recycle bin on the aft deck, and returned to her repair job. Running her fingers over the paint, she assessed her work. For now, the scraping was done. She dug in her supplies for the wood filler. It irked her the gouge was deep enough that it had to be filled. Not for the first time, she wished the hole Joe's absence had left in her life could be filled as easily. With a small plastic bowl and wooden paint stick, she added powder and water until she figured she had enough mixture at the right consistency then, with a light touch, carefully applied the first layer. In the humidity, it was better to layer it in than fill it completely first round.

"Ms. Devon?"

Startled, Dawn leaned back on her stool and almost fell backwards. Regaining her balance, she sprang to a standing position. "Who's asking?"

"Ms. Devon, I'm Shorty. I'm working down the dock on the Kontiki Dreamer." The squat man, true to his name, stuck his hand out. She held out her palms, dirty from working and shrugged. "Her owner mentioned you might have some repairs to be done here." Shorty's eyes drifted to her bucket of supplies, the putty knife in her hand, and the repair on the hull. "Jeez, that's an ugly gash."

"'Tis," she said. "Bozo scraped in along the side of us."

"I can have that looking good as new in a few hours."

"I've already made a start on it."

Shorty held his hand up. "You're doing a fine job. Sorry to have bothered you." He turned to go.

"By a few hours, what do you have in mind?" Dawn could have kicked herself. She didn't have the money for the repair, but it galled her that the Papa Joe might end up looking like a patched up old tub. Joe's legacy deserved better.

Turning back, Shorty said, "Three. Four tops."

Together they looked at the hull and the first layer of filler in the crevice.

"What's your hourly?"

"Forty-five."

She felt her eyes widen and quickly reset her features. "Oh, that won't—"

"I'm the best detailer around. Ask anyone."

"I don't doubt that, it's only—"

"This was Joe Black's boat, was it not?"

"It was." She hooked her right thumb through a belt loop on her shorts.

"He was a good man," Shorty said, his eyes sliding down the hull toward the bow.

"He was."

Shorty returned his gaze to her. "I did a little work for him in the past. I liked Joe. I'll give you a flat rate of a hundred bucks."

"That's only a little over two hours," Dawn said. "Why would you do that?"

"Like I said, I liked Joe. I can get to it tomorrow if you like, once I'm done over at the Serenity Jane."

Dawn tried to read his face and failed. He didn't look like a man out scrounging for work, but he'd dropped his rate fast. Still, many people had been genuinely kind following Joe's death. She'd love to have the repair properly done. The cash in the coffee can in the galley, the last of her savings--barely enough to get groceries--would cover the repair. She'd had nothing before and lived through it. She blew off the anxiety and extended her hand to seal the deal, but as she did she spotted the marina store manager making his way down the dock toward them. He didn't look happy and he had someone else following hot on his heels.

Knowing what was coming, Dawn backpedaled quickly. "Shorty, that's very generous. Can I come round and talk to you about it tomorrow? I just realized I forgot an appointment."

Cocking one brow, he turned toward shore and saw the two men barreling down the dock. "Doesn't look like your appointment will be happy to be kept waiting. Tomorrow then." He tipped his chin and walked off.

"Shorty," the store manager greeted him.

"Jeff", Shorty said.

Dawn leaned back against the hull in the shade and waited for the shit to hit the proverbial fan.

CHAPTER SIX

Dawn tapped her short, chipped nails against the boat, praying to the water gods for inspiration, as Jeff and the second man drew closer to her slip. Part of the reputation she'd earned in the ring had been for her quick thinking. Why the hell was it failing her now? These days, more often than not, she froze rather than fought.

"Dawn." Jeff greeted her, his face a study in conflicted emotions with apology in the forefront. "This here is my boss, Mr. Smith, the new General Manager of the marina."

The General Manager, decked out in a linen suit, skinny black tie and white shoes, appeared to be trying a little too hard. When he opened his mouth, his New York accent betrayed him completely, and she remembered Joe bitching about new management and how it would change things.

"Ms. Devon, nice to meet you. Let me say how sorry I am for your loss. I only met Mr. Black once in passing, but he seemed a decent type." A tall, lean man, with hair the color of his suit, his mouth moved with exaggerated motion, like a Mr. Potato Head figure.

"You could say that," Dawn said, leaning forward to shake

the hand he extended. His hand was clammy, his shake limp. She resisted the urge to wipe her palm against her shorts.

He leaned back on his heels and shoved his hands in his pockets. A bead of sweat carved a trail downward from his temple. "Look, I don't want to be a hard ass, and I know things have been tough during this... transition period. At the same time, we do feel the marina management has been more than fair with you." He glanced to Jeff for support.

Jeff only shrugged his shoulders. "As you asked, I told her the end of the week."

Smith turned back to Dawn. "Right, and here we are on a Friday afternoon."

"I have most of the moorage," Dawn lied, thinking of the hundred bucks she'd already tagged for Shorty and her half-finished repair. "I guess I was figuring the end of the week for tomorrow."

"Tomorrow's Saturday." He unbuttoned his jacket. Vanity was a funny thing. She was suffering in shorts and tank top, yet he wore a full suit on the dock. Linen or not, it had to be hot.

She jammed her hands in her pockets, stood straight and squared her shoulders. "Technically the end of the week."

The man blinked twice, slanted a look at Jeff and stepped back a couple of inches. "I don't want to be unreasonable here. Would you like to pay us what you do have now, and the balance tomorrow?"

"Well, the problem is..." she paused, searching for inspiration, and her eye fell on the long shadow she cast on the deck. "I'd have to get to the bank." She shrugged. "It would be closed for now."

"Can you get there tomorrow?" His eyes narrowed. Despite his appearance, he clearly had a good nose for bullshit.

"Well... "

"Banks in these parts will be closed tomorrow," Jeff said, trying to suppress a smile. "Can we give Dawn until Monday?

No harm done, right? There's nobody in the office tomorrow anyway."

"You'll be in the office tomorrow," Mr. Smith said. "You can accept the payment."

"Like Jeff said, I can't get to the bank now until Monday." She took a breath and tried to appear humbler, or at least less confrontational. What she needed was a little more time, to give him enough confidence in her so she could stall a couple more days. To what end, she didn't know, but at this moment the only thing she had on her side was time.

"I'd sure appreciate it." She flashed him a smile, willing her eyes to smile along with her mouth, while fear and anger snaked through her insides. She hated the feeling of being up against the wall, and under someone else's thumb.

Smith exhaled a big sigh, and shook his head, his carefully orchestrated expression falling away to reveal his regard of her as some form of lesser human, as if all liveaboards were beach bums and boat rats.

His gaze dropped beside her left leg, at the fill still drying on the hull. "You doing this repair yourself?"

She shrugged. "Best I can. Can't afford anyone else to take care of it."

"Wasn't the guy you were talking with when we arrived the guy who does boat repairs?" His nose practically twitched. She was reminded of a washed-out rabbit or Bewitched.

"Shorty. I told him I didn't have the cash to hire him. Mostly, he came 'round to offer his condolences." She dropped her gaze to the deck for effect, desperate to send the General Manager on his way.

"Monday then," he said, relenting. He clawed at a strand of hair plastered to his humid forehead. "But I expect to see you in the office before the end of day, no excuses."

Dawn nodded and forced out the words, "I'll be there."

"Let's go, Jeff." The big boss turned tail and walked back up the deck, his fine linen jacket flapping behind him. The only thing missing to complete his resemblance to the White Rabbit was the lack of a pocket watch and him mumbling about being late.

It should have made her laugh but her mood remained grim, her vulnerability simmering so close to the surface she couldn't tap into her sense of humor.

CHAPTER SEVEN

BELOW DECK, TUCKED INTO THE BERTH IN THE BOW, DAWN shook the last of the chip crumbs out of the large family-sized bag she'd demolished watching reruns of Dexter, and tossed them in her mouth. She discarded the bag on top of the other junk food and candy wrappers piled on top of the dirty plates on the other berth.

She'd lost track of the hours, filling her time with television and food to keep her mind from delving into the truly dark side of her psyche that was fighting for attention. She had no money and nowhere to go. She'd started a list of places she might look for work then crossed off each idea. With no skills, no work experience, and nobody to vouch for her, she had little hope of picking up a job in the next 48 hours. Even if she could, they'd be unlikely to immediately advance enough of her pay to cover the nut the marina wanted.

One thing she hadn't considered was offering to work for them. She dropped the candy bar she was unwrapping, and added that to the list along with a big question mark. For good measure, she doodled a little lightbulb, tracing the lines repeatedly until the lead snapped.

A sign. Why would they hire a barely clean broken-down boxer with nothing to offer? Still, at the moment, it was the best idea she had. She hugged her knees up to her chest and muted the volume on the commercials. A phone rang.

Her phone? She couldn't be sure, it was from somewhere at least a few feet away. In any case, she had zero intention of talking to anyone today. Maybe not tomorrow either. The show came back on and she killed the mute button. She let the images anesthetize her back into a zone and rifled among the bed covers for the half-opened candy bar.

More commercials. She really needed satellite, cause the local cable sucked eggs. Although, the chance of the marina upgrading her utility package when she couldn't pay moorage was pretty much nil. Grabbing the remote, she muted the volume.

The phone was ringing. Again or still? She wasn't sure. Why hadn't she simply turned the damn thing off? She turned the TV volume back up, despite the commercials, before curiosity got the best of her. Ditching the remote on the berth, she went in search of the phone.

Crossing the wheelhouse, she assessed the time of day to be late afternoon, sliding into who-gives-a-shit o'clock. The sun shone brightly in through the large front wheelhouse windows. Last night she'd closed everything up tight and the air was close and hot as hell. The phone continued ringing.

Stepping down into the galley, she spotted the offending hunk of electronics on the table, scooped it up, and hit 'Ignore call' as fast as she could. The ringing was vibrating through her bones and edging out the fragile morsel of peace she'd cultivated.

The screen flashed seven missed calls, all from the same number. Someone was insistent. The number was unknown to her. Her finger hovered over the button to return the call, but the squeezing sensation in her chest increased so instead she turned the cell off and tossed it back on the table. It skipped three times before it slid into the ledge that ran along the edge and stopped. A five-hundred-dollar phone and she couldn't care less.

Rummaging in the fridge, she found two more cans of soda, a container of leftover fried rice, and another of sweet and sour chicken. Prying the tops off the takeout containers, she subjected it all to the sniff test. Good enough. She grabbed a fork and the drinks and headed back toward her lair down below.

As she passed through the wheelhouse, someone called her name. She ducked.

"Dawn, it's Timothy."

Damn, had he seen her?

"Hey, I need your help with something. I know you're in there."

Crouched in the middle of the wheelhouse floor, feeling more than a little ridiculous, she held her breath. She should stand up. Tell him to piss off and leave her alone. But so far she'd managed to maintain a thread of social graces in the marina and she wasn't going to blow that now. If she had to, she'd wait him out.

Timothy banged twice on the port door before cursing and walking back down the dock.

Heaving a sigh of relief, she rose, walked to the stairs and returned to her bunk. Maybe the calls had been from him? How would he get her number? Did he even know she had a phone?

That's when it hit her. Of course. The phone. She could put an ad on Craigslist and get a couple hundred bucks. Maybe more. She'd do it first thing in the morning.

If that didn't pan out, she'd pawn it.

The only people she wanted to speak to hadn't called in over two years.

CHAPTER EIGHT

Sunday morning the light slanting in through the hatch hit Dawn straight in the eyes. She rolled over, dragging the pillow over her head, and went back to sleep. Some hours later, she woke up in a sauna, kicking the bed covers onto the floor. The sun had moved on, past the hatch, and judging from the heat in the cabin, the day was far advanced.

Her head pounded from the overdose of sugar, her clothes clung to her skin in the crushing heat, and her teeth wore little sweaters. After all the junk food and bad TV, she'd fallen asleep without brushing her teeth. Swearing, she swung her legs out of bed, put her feet firmly on the floor, and stumbled to the head. Why not be hung over if she was going to feel this bad?

She regarded herself in the mirror. The girl in the glass knew the answer to that. She knew where she'd been last night and could be certain nobody was hunting her for some trouble she'd gotten up to. After relieving herself, she ran her hands under the tap, then grabbed her toothbrush and scrubbed for a good five minutes. When she was done, her tongue glided easily over the enamel and she exposed her teeth to the mirror. Good enough.

Her stomach rumbled. Real food would do her good. Aside from the questionable leftover Chinese food, all she'd had yesterday was candy and chips. In the galley, she lit the burner under a cast iron pan and fried up the last of the bacon and a couple of eggs.

On the aft deck, looking out over the sea, she tucked into the meal with gusto. On Sundays, the harbor was dotted with pleasure craft from the marina to the south. Large Chris-Crafts and sleek sailboats glided peacefully over the top of the waves.

After mopping the yolk off the plate with her toast, she popped the last remaining piece of crisp bacon into her mouth, savoring the flavor on her tongue. Damned if bacon didn't make everything better.

Back in the galley, she poured a coffee, slid onto the bench at the table and picked up her phone. Three more missed calls. All the same number. She deleted the notifications.

Opening her browser, she surfed over to Craigslist and posted the ad for the phone. Her finger hovered over the Post button. It was only a phone. She needed the cash and she could get another one. She pushed the button and the screen froze. She waited. A warning flashed that her data had expired and she could buy more.

In what world could she buy more? Disgusted, she flung the phone on the table, stalked down to the forward cabin and threw on a fresh pair of shorts and the closest shirt she could get her hands on.

"Hey, Dawn." Timothy's voice floated in through the port-hole. Was the little shit spying on her or what?

"Seriously Dawn," he whined, "can we talk for a few minutes?"

Sighing, she pushed the hatch off and poked her head out. "Can't it wait, Timothy?"

He peered up at her, his face freshly shaven and eyes clear. A new look for him. "It really can't."

She pushed herself out of the hatch and sat cross-legged on the edge of the forward cabin.

"I had the mechanic over the other day."

"I saw that."

"It didn't go well. Cost me a bundle and he pronounced the motor tits up." He grimaced. "Sorry for the language."

She'd heard a lot worse in the ring, and in the bars, but he didn't need to know that. "Sorry to hear that."

"Well, here's the thing. I have a charter coming up at the end of the week and if I cancel it I won't have the money to fix the engine. It's sort of a chicken and egg situation."

"Sounds like a worry, for sure," she said. She held her breath, knowing if he asked for money she could immediately say no, without a speck of guilt, because she didn't have two pennies to rub together.

"I noticed Jeff and the new General Manager stopped by the other day" he said. She leaned back, not liking the direction the conversation was taking. Her business was her business. She valued her privacy which was a difficult thing to maintain in such close quarters. "They paid me a little visit."

"You haven't paid your moorage," he stated.

Her eyes narrowed, and she felt a hardening inside her. "That's not really any of your business." She pushed off the deck and started to stand.

"No, wait," he pleaded, holding a hand up. "Shit, I didn't mean it like that. I just meant, maybe we can help each other."

"I don't see how." Dawn slid her legs down the hatch. She perched on the edge, itching to end the conversation by disappearing below.

"What if I could show you a way we'd both get what we need?"

Interest piqued, she raised her chin. "What do you mean?"

"So the charter, it's a course for a bunch of wannabe sailors. Not sailors, exactly, but folks who have never spent much time on a boat. Folks with deep pockets." He paused to let that sink in. "What if we take 'em out in your boat? I won't have to cancel the charter and you'll make enough coin to pay the moorage, and then some."

Dawn's eyes dropped, almost involuntarily, past Timothy's clean-shaven face to the filthy T-shirt he wore atop dirty, baggy khakis. She couldn't imagine him being front man for anything.

"This something you've done before, Timothy?"

He shrugged and met her eyes. "I used to have a partner. I haven't run one in a while, not since she left, but somehow these folks still had my number."

She? Timothy had had a partner who was a she? Good god, she should go back to bed, the whole world was tipping on its axis.

CHAPTER NINE

Dawn hated to quash the hopefulness on Timothy's face as he stood gazing up at her but the thought of spending a full day with him made it easy to say what she did next.

"It wouldn't work Timothy, but thanks for considering me."

"No." He stamped his foot on the dock. "We're two people, both of us about to lose our boats—"

"Well, I don't know that we're about to lose our boats. I mean, you'll come up with the money you need for the engine, and I'll—"

"No," he said again. "This course is happening in a few days. If I lose this charter, things are gonna be grim for me. I barely get by. And by the look of things, Dawn," he looked straight at her as his eyes narrowed, "you're barely getting by yourself."

"Listen, I'm not right for this," she said. "I'm still learning myself. Come on, you know Joe was a good teacher, but I'm not ready to teach anything to anybody."

Timothy sensed an opening and edged closer. "You won't have to. I'll do all the teaching. You just have to captain the boat."

"You say that like it's an easy thing."

"I'll help. I'll be your first mate. There isn't a thing I don't know about boats."

"Except how to fix your engine." The instant the words were out of her mouth she regretted them. Hurt and rage twisted his features. He settled with rage and sneered back at her.

"At least I'm looking for solutions. You're just hiding from the world hoping your problems will go away."

Anger flared through her. "Right now, I'm just hoping you'll go away." With that she slid into the forward cabin, pulling the hatch closed behind her.

"You know it's a good idea, Dawn," Timothy yelled. "It'll help both of us." He slapped his hand against the hull. "Freakin' hard-headed woman. Lose this boat and Joe will roll over in his damn grave."

He stomped off without another word. Nothing more was necessary, he'd already sucker punched her. She doubled over, the truth of his words an arrow of grief in her gut.

———

For the rest of the afternoon, Dawn wandered through downtown Merritt looking for WiFi to upload her Craigslist ad and sell her phone. There were plenty of options if she wanted to sit down and eat somewhere or pay for an overpriced coffee. She snorted. Coffee. Why not call it what it was? A fancy liquid desert served hot.

She'd stalked off as soon as Timothy had left, and in her haste hadn't bothered to bring cash. Not that she had much to bring. So not only could she not buy data, she also couldn't eat. It seemed like every bistro and cafe within walking distance was filled to the brim with families, couples and groups of friends enjoying late lunches.

After striking out on the main street, she crossed two blocks over until she reached the small Public Library. They'd have WiFi. A teenaged couple, wrapped around each other, sat at the top of the stairs. She breezed past them to the front door but when she pulled the latch, the door stayed in place.

"Closed Sundays," said the girl, over her young lover's shoulder.

"Thanks." Dawn stared at the schedule posted in the window. Closed Sunday.

Not sure where to head next, she wandered along the back streets hoping to pick up an unsecured signal. She loitered in front of a couple of houses until a man mowing his lawn came over to ask if she was lost.

Embarrassed and out of ideas, she took the shortest route back to the marina. She was hungry again.

She walked down the dock, praying she could avoid a second run-in with Timothy, and resigning herself to a supper of more eggs.

CHAPTER TEN

Monday morning Dawn hit the library steps as the door was being unlocked. She waited patiently while an elderly man shuffled through the door ahead of her. Standing in the lobby, she took a minute to get her bearings. Although the library was walking distance from her old apartment, she'd never been in it before. The building was a clean, simple design with good bones, a high ceiling and plenty of natural light. When the woman at the desk asked if she'd like to become a member, she signed up for a temporary card as a visitor.

Making her way to a study table in a quiet corner, she posted the Craigslist ad, checked her email, and muted her phone when it rang. Same caller. Again. She hit *Ignore* and considered blocking the number.

With the listing uploaded, she did a google search of businesses nearby cross-referencing the list she'd made the day before and taking screenshots as she sifted through them. The small space got noisier as more people filed in, chatted with others, returned books, asked for their holds. Before long, the walls started to close in on her.

She stepped back into the late-morning sun and ran through

a short list of businesses in her head. She would ask for work. If she couldn't come up with the cash for tomorrow, at least she could show she was trying. For now, it was the best she could do.

Business after business turned her down. They were polite enough. Most of them. She presented well, but when it came down to it, they weren't hiring and she didn't have a skill to offer them. Her final stop was a Greek restaurant a few blocks from her old place, which was not the greatest part of town. Kind of a seedy looking joint, she'd often passed by their sidewalk sign announcing Souvlaki and Greek salad lunch specials. Today, she marched up to the door and let herself inside.

After the calm of the sidewalk, the din of the dining area was overwhelming. Two waiters scurried between tables, run off their feet by the lunch crowd. Every table was filled. One of the waiters said he'd be with her in a minute. She waited over ten, the skin under her collar growing warmer by the second, before deciding she'd have to come back another time. Or she could slip on an apron and help out. Like that was going to happen.

Still, something needed to happen. She pushed out the front door and hurried down the street. At the corner, she hung a right until she hit the alley and hung another right to circle to the back of the restaurant. The alley, a mix of residential and commercial, was surprisingly well kept. It offered peek-a-boo looks into well-trimmed back yards filled with large palm trees, bird baths and feeders, well-tended flower beds. Bright bougainvillea in pink, white, and mauve trailed down back gates and fences, their papery petals a rainbow of confetti along the pavement.

It didn't take long to hone in on the restaurant. A large dumpster stood near the propped back door, and a burly man in a sweat-stained wife-beater leaned against the door jamb. His eye slid over her like a well-greased egg sliding onto a plate.

She bit her tongue and focused on why she was here. "The boss around?"

"Busy."

"I only need to speak to him for a minute."

"Lunch time." As if that was all the explanation necessary, he took a long drag off what was left of his cigarette and flicked the butt into the alley.

"Maybe I'll just come in and find his office."

"Yeah, you do that." The man expelled a harsh laugh, turning his wide back to her as he returned inside.

The air glimmered by the kitchen door as the sweltering heat poured into the afternoon humidity outside. The kitchen was hopping. She spotted at least eight people, all in perpetual, frantic motion. To the far right, the double door opened and one of the waiters stepped in. The dining room entrance. She turned her attention to the left and spotted an open door along a small hallway across from the large walk-in refrigerator.

Without consulting anyone, she walked toward it and tapped on the doorframe. The owner, head down going through paperwork, glared up at her through a shock of thick, white hair that hung over his broad forehead. "No appointments until after three," he grunted.

"I just need—"

"A minute? That's what they all say." He rose to his feet, a man of ample girth, and started around the edge of his desk. "Who let you in here?"

Dawn could feel any chance she might have slipping away, so she blurted out the rest as fast as possible. "I'm not selling anything. I need a job."

His grey eyes focused on her from below bushy brows. "Don't need a waitress."

"Maybe a hostess?"

He laughed. It was a deep, warm belly laugh out of sync with the look on his face. "In this joint? Hon, we're full up," he said.

He was warming up to her, so she pressed on. "Someone to do cleaning? Or take care of paperwork?" She waved her hand toward the mess on his desk. "I could do the filing, help with the books."

"You a bookkeeper? I got one but she's retiring soon. Did she send you?"

"No, I... but I can learn. I'm good with numbers," she lied.

The openness in his face faded and he moved his bulk toward the door. "Look, hon, I'm sorry but I don't have anything for you right now."

She started to back out of the office into the din of the kitchen but desperation made her stop and plant her feet. He advanced until he was practically toe to toe, his large frame looming over her.

"Anything," she pleaded. "I can do prep in the kitchen or clear tables. Even wash dishes."

Suddenly the air in the kitchen grew heavy and time stopped in a bubble of silence.

"You want Mario's job?" A smile twerked at the corner of the owner's lip.

"You want *my* job?"

Dawn turned. The booming voice belonged to the big man from the alley, his hands plunged into suds above his elbows to his well-inked upper arms, each as wide around as one of her thighs. If he wasn't an ex-con, she was born yesterday.

He took his hands out of the water and placed his fists on his hips, water dripping onto the grimy linoleum beneath his feet. "You want my job?"

"Sorry, hon," the owner continued. "Like I said, I've got nothing for you."

Dawn stumbled through the laughter of the kitchen staff, slipping on the floor as she passed one of the stainless counters, and almost losing her balance. The laughter increased and she propelled herself out the door, back into the alley and ran down the small lane toward the street. On the way out, the pretty fences flashed by in a blur, closing in on her as she raced past.

When she stepped back onto the curb, she felt more hopeless than she had on Saturday. More boxed in than she had on Sunday. And more of a mess than she had in some time. A tear squeezed from her eye.

She'd never missed Joe so much as at this moment.

CHAPTER ELEVEN

On Tuesday morning, Dawn lay in bed. With each creak of the lines and shifting of the dock, she started, expecting Jeff or Smith or both to pound on the doors and insist she pay up. Several minutes later, sick of herself, she swung out of bed, pulled some shorts on and made her way to the galley.

After starting a strong pot of coffee, she opened the fridge, grimaced at the two eggs left in the little plastic holder on the door and slammed the door shut. Rifling through the cupboard above, she spied an old package of oatmeal with barely enough oats left to feed her. She dumped the contents into a small pot, shaking the bag to be sure she got it all, added water and put it on the burner next to the percolator.

The window over the stove looked out the port side toward the dock. Beyond the boat across from her, the sky was a rich blue, wisps of clouds skittering across it like kittens chasing each other's tails. Or like smoke, as her life went up in freaking flames.

Despite the reason for her newfound ownership on the boat, and the crushing grief, in some ways the last few weeks had been among the most peaceful of her life. Rocking gently to sleep on the waves at night suited her. Her bohemian and primarily reclusive neighbors suited her. She hated to give it all up.

Giving the oatmeal a quick stir, she turned the coffee pot to low and poured a cup, sitting at the table to check her phone. Two more missed calls from the unknown caller. Now her curiosity was piqued.

Sliding a pen and piece of paper toward her, she scratched out some notes. More ideas on how she could scrounge up the money she needed, each more far-fetched than the one before. She took a sip of coffee, regarded the list and, one by one, crossed the ideas off, not sure whether she should attribute the pounding in her chest to rising anxiety or caffeine.

"Dawn."

She checked the time. Three minutes after nine. Time to face the music.

With a firm grip on her mug, she stepped out the galley door onto the back deck.

"Hey, morning Dawn," Shorty said, all smiles, "I came by to see you on Saturday, but I guess I missed you." Shorty set his tool box and bucket of supplies onto the dock. "I thought I'd get started on that repair while it's still cool."

It was anything but cool, the sun already high over the horizon. "Yeah, sorry I missed you, Shorty." She stepped down onto the dock beside him. "Not much shade here for working right now."

"That's fine," he said. "Better for me to get started, then I can leave things to dry and come back later in the day to finish things off."

"You'll finish it all today?"

He shrugged. "Most likely, the filler at least. I'll have to come back another day for the fine sanding and to touch up the paint." He leaned forward and ran his finger along the gouge, almost a caress. "That work for you?"

There was less money now than when she'd made the deal with him. "Shorty, I probably can't pay you the whole thing right away."

"Don't worry," he said. "Pay when I'm done." His eyes dropped to the mug in her hand and his smile widened. "You could ply me with caffeine."

"Shit, sorry, of course. Let me grab you a cup." Dawn returned to the galley, turned off the oatmeal that was bubbling into a glutinous, unappetizing looking mess, and grabbed a coffee for Shorty. "Cream? Sugar?" she shouted out the back door.

"Black."

Good thing. While there was probably some sugar somewhere, there sure as hell wasn't cream, or even milk or that horrible powdered creamer Joe had favored.

She stepped back outside. Shorty had already stretched out a tarp along the side of the pier and was assembling the first tools he'd need. "Here you go."

He reached up for the cup, nodded his head, and went back to his work. It felt like a dismissal, which suited her fine.

"If you need anything, let me know."

"You bet." A man of few needs and fewer words. Even better.

Back in the galley, she scooped the oatmeal--now the consistency of drying cement--into a plastic bowl, sorry she didn't have milk. She dug through the cupboards, found the last of the sugar, and poured a few clumps into the mess. Hungry, she ate it all.

CHAPTER TWELVE

A LITTLE AFTER ELEVEN, COLORFUL CURSES RANG THROUGH the air from somewhere down the dock. From the top deck, where she was painting some trim, she turned. Timothy was heavy into an argument with the mechanic. Didn't he say the other day that the engine was dead? Was he trying to bring it back to life? The little zombie engine that could. She chuckled then felt bad laughing at his misfortune.

The mechanic yelled back, gathered his tool chest and jumped off the stern of Timothy's boat. "I won't be back."

"Don't worry, I don't want to see your face back here ever." Timothy's face was an unhealthy red, his fists balled at his side.

"Lose my number," the mechanic shouted back over his shoulder as he strode down the pier toward shore.

"Yeah... yeah, well... last word freak!" yelled Timothy. Dawn stifled another laugh and lowered her head as he turned in her direction. She waited. After a few seconds, she snuck a peek, but Timothy had returned back inside. A string of sour language streamed out accompanied by metal slamming on metal, and the sound of the large engine doors being dropped closed. Then, nothing.

Dawn stood and peeked over the edge to the dock. "How's it going, Shorty? Can I get you anything?"

He looked up from one knee, his head bent close to the hull. "Almost done for now," he said. "I'll wrap up and be back in a few hours. Mind if I leave my bucket on the stern while I'm gone?"

"No problem," Dawn said. "I'll be here all day." Not that anyone would board the boat in broad daylight and steal anything, but she wanted to add some caveat. She didn't know how she was going to pay him, let alone replace missing tools.

"Miss Devon."

Dawn glanced to the left. Jeff and Smith were making their way down the pier. Despite the last few days of worry, she rolled her shoulders back and raised her chin, ready for the fight. *Bring it.*

"I was expecting to see you in the office yesterday," Mr. Smith said. Behind him, Jeff shrugged his shoulder, palms up.

"I was out," she said, looking down at him.

"I waited until after 8 pm."

She shrugged. She'd avoided him until 9 pm, hanging around the park in the center of town but he didn't have to know that.

"We had an agreement," Mr. Smith said. He crossed his arms, his light blue linen suit bunching at the shoulders as he did. Perched on the dock, he reminded her of a great blue heron. Gawky and looking for prey.

"I was out looking for work," she said. "I picked up a part-time job."

"Did they pay you in advance?" Mr. Smith quirked a brow. Sarcasm dripped off his words thicker than the late morning air.

Dawn bit her tongue. At this moment, Smith held all the power. And she hated that. She measured her next words, careful with her tone. "I'm afraid not," she said. "But I'll have your money by the end of the week."

He shook his head. "That's not good enough." He turned

and pointed toward Shorty. "Apparently you have enough money to repair your boat but not enough to moor it?"

Shorty looked up, then pushed to a standing position. "I'm doing Dawn a favor." He had to look up at Smith, but there was no warmth in his eyes. "Joe was a good friend and I'm helping Dawn out. Not that it's any of your business."

Dawn made a mental note to thank Shorty, maybe with a big tip. Smith looked from Shorty to Dawn. "I hope that's the truth of it."

"Why would he lie?" Dawn put her hands on her hips. "I'm getting kind of tired of your attitude," she said.

"Ms. Devon," Mr. Smith said, "you will pay your fees by the end of the day or we'll have to ask you to leave the marina."

Dawn's head swiveled as she heard footsteps along the pier. Great. The situation was sliding from bad to worse. Timothy inserted himself between the two men, sticking his hand out to Smith. "We haven't met officially," he said, clearly eager to ingratiate himself. "I'm Timothy Tyler Talbert. I was also a friend of Joe's."

The General Manager looked at Timothy's grimy hand and cocked his head.

Timothy continued. "I've been talking with Dawn about this and I believe we've come up with a solution."

Dawn hustled down the ladder at the back and stood on the stern, trying to catch Timothy's eye. He studiously ignored her.

"Is that so? Do tell," he said, studying Timothy like wildlife he hadn't come across before. Or roadkill on his shoe.

"I'm having a little engine trouble," he said, "but I have a charter coming up. So, Dawn and I are going to do the charter on the Papa Joe. She'll be able to pay the moorage from the proceeds."

Mr. Smith's brow creased as he looked over at Dawn. "I thought you said you'd picked up a part-time job?"

She shielded her eyes against the sun and shrugged. "I did. I wanted to cover all the bases."

Beside Smith, Timothy grinned like the cat who caught the canary. Damn him.

Shorty had finished packing up his things and stood off to the side, watching things play out.

Smith turned briefly to Timothy, then fixed Dawn in a stare. "This better not be more bullshit."

"It's true," Timothy said. "We're doing the charter together and then she can pay you."

Dawn looked over at Timothy. He was throwing her a life line, she was smart enough to see that, even if it was self-serving. Being in Shorty's debt was one thing, but being in Timothy's?

"No, it's bullshit," she said. A hush fell over them. Smith's brows shot up. "I haven't agreed to anything. But like I told you, I picked up a part-time job and I can pay you by week's end."

Smith shook his head. "Not good enough. You've had enough warnings. See us in the office by the end of the day or you're out." He pursed his lips, threw her a look of disgust, and turned heel. Jeff frowned at Dawn and followed his boss up the pier.

Timothy stood in the middle of Shorty's tarp staring up at her. "You are one hard-headed b—"

"Boater?" Shorty cut him off. "She's one hard-headed boater? Maybe she doesn't like other people planning out her life for her."

Timothy's jaw dropped.

Kicking at the corner of his tarp, Shorty said, "Mind moving off my tarp so I can pack up?"

"You'll be sorry about this," Timothy said, shooting a look at Dawn. "I'm just trying to help you out." He stomped away.

"Help himself out is more like it," Shorty said in a low voice.

Dawn hopped onto the deck and shook Shorty's hand. "Thanks for your help. I wasn't expecting that."

"Well, it was bullshit," he said, with a grin. "You'll still have to pay me."

"I plan to," Dawn said.

"When you can," he said. "Deal with the marina first. I can wait a couple weeks." He tilted his chin down the dock. "If you do get involved with Timothy for the charter, be sure to watch your back. He's a slippery one."

CHAPTER THIRTEEN

LATER THAT NIGHT, STRETCHED OUT ON HER BUNK, watching Double Jeopardy for at least the tenth time, Dawn's anxiety was abated with a small sense of satisfaction that she'd kept the wolf from the door. If only for a little while. She hit the remote as the commercials came on and heard her phone ringing in the galley. Again she'd forgotten to turn it off. She couldn't wait to be rid of it. In the morning, she'd go back to the library to see if anyone had responded to the Craigslist ad.

Turning back to her show, she hit the remote but nothing happened, the screen had gone black. She changed the channel. Nothing. Hit the power button off, back on again. Still nothing. Turning the remote over, she removed the batteries, then reseated them and tried again. No luck.

She needed to check the connection. The sun had set almost an hour ago, and the dim light streaming through the window from the pier lights wasn't enough, so she leaned over and flipped the switch for the overhead light.

Nothing.

Feeling her way over to one of the cubby holes, she grabbed a flash light and guided herself up the stairs to the master switch panel. A quick check revealed everything in order. She switched the power over to 12 volt and turned a couple of lights on.

Stepping out on the stern, she could hear strains of music and television noises from the other boats nearby. Everyone else still had power. Jumping down onto the deck, she checked her shore line and found a note. *Sorry it came to this. See us in the office first thing in the morning.- Jeff.*

They'd shut off her power. She stood on the dock, arms crossed and looked out to sea. The small bit of satisfaction and relief she'd been feeling floated away on the evening breeze. A large trawler was silhouetted against the horizon, where a thin line of purple stood guard against the dying light.

A white light in her belly started to spread and she took a deep breath. Getting upset wouldn't help her focus on the immediate problem. She took inventory. She had 12 volt for the lights. The stove and fridge ran on propane. There was so little in the fridge she could almost turn it off. Basically the shore power just saved her batteries and allowed her to use the larger electronics.

The line in the sand had been drawn.

She tossed and turned through the long night, her mind too busy to sleep. Solutions eluded her.

The prospect of being homeless hung over her head. Money should motivate her but after the disaster of the last charter, it did not. As the only witness to Joe's death, she was determined to be available when it came time for the hearing. She couldn't simply disappear.

And then there was Timothy himself. Joe had disliked him intensely. He definitely rubbed her the wrong way. Even Shorty had warned her about him. Surely Timothy would not be her only way out of this.

CHAPTER FOURTEEN

D awn woke feeling like the largest boxer she'd ever fought was kneeling on her shoulders. She sat up and gulped in air, pushing the dream and weight off. Her eye took in the small cabin, the place she'd been calling home. She didn't have much. A shelf of old John D. MacDonald paperbacks, a few Alfred Hitchcock magazines, and some rain gear. A few changes of clothes. It wouldn't take long to throw it all in a gym bag and move on to the next spot.

But where would that next spot be? And why would she walk away from the home Joe had wanted her to have. She wanted to stay and fight but she'd run out of options. She could sit in the boat until they took the next step. She couldn't imagine what that would be. The minute the boat left the slip, or she left the boat, she was certain they'd take some action to bar her from returning.

Feeling beat down, she took a few minutes in the head to prepare herself for the day. In the galley, the phone was already ringing. It was barely 7 a.m. She went to the galley to make coffee and checked the screen. Same number. She rolled her eyes. *Same shit, different day*.

The sun was already above the horizon, gulls circled a fishing boat coming in through the mouth of the harbor, a small fish jumped in the bay a few feet off the starboard side. Her head pounded. Joe would kill her if she lost his boat for a reason as stupid as this.

Not that the boat was in danger. It was legally hers. She could always just sail out to sea and drop anchor somewhere. If she had money for diesel that could be an option. And money for food. She'd only exist so long on a handful of old eggs.

A footfall on the pier caught her attention and she peeked out the window but didn't have the right angle to see who it was.

"Dawn."

She stayed silent.

"Dawn, it's Thomas Duncan."

Joe's lawyer? She cracked the galley door. Duncan stood on the pier, dressed in a pin-striped navy suit, an expensive-looking burgundy leather briefcase dangling from his right hand. "Mr. Duncan, what are you doing here?"

"I've been trying to reach you for days," he said. "Did you lose your phone?"

"Uh, no," she said, glancing over her shoulder at her cell on the table. "I just got out of bed, give me a minute to get dressed."

"Be quick about it," he said sharply, glancing at the Cartier on his wrist. "I'm on my way to court."

Geez. Pushy much? Dawn hustled down to the forward cabin, threw on a cleaner T-shirt and a pair of khakis, returned through the galley and out onto the stern. Duncan raised his brow.

"Want to come aboard for a coffee?" she asked, pushing aside her earlier annoyance.

"Thanks, no time today. Come on down, will you?" She

stepped up on deck, then down onto the dock, landing lightly at his side.

He shifted his briefcase to his left side and extended his hand, which she shook. "Nice to see you, Dawn."

"And you, Mr. Duncan," she said, her mind racing a mile a minute wondering why he would have been so insistent on reaching her. "I think," she added.

"Thomas," he said. "Mr. Duncan makes me look around for my father. Look, Dawn, I don't want to alarm you but the hearing for the divers is coming up soon."

"For Nico and Mark, you mean?"

"Right, somehow it escaped my paralegal's eye on the schedule and I just found out about it on Saturday."

Dawn's chest clenched. Saturday coincided with the beginning of the missed phone calls. "I'm glad you let me know," she said. "I want to be there for that."

"You misunderstand me," he said, pushing his hand back through his hair. "There's no need to be at the hearing. It's a formality. But the point is, the Cubans and perhaps the head guy who set up the charter with Joe—"

"Dylan?"

"Right. The thing is, they're likely to be in town during the hearing."

Her muscles tightened up and down her spine. "All the more reason to be there," she said. "I definitely want to see those bastards again."

"Dawn." Duncan put his hand up in a stop motion and glanced, not so subtly, at the time again. The crystal of the Cartier sparked in the morning sun. "It would be highly dangerous for you to be there. You're the only witness to Joe's death. I came to tell you to get away for a few days."

"I can't do that."

"Just a few days. Go visit a friend in Key Largo. If you stay here on the boat, you'll be an easy target."

"No, I mean... " She hesitated, her cheeks heating.

"What is it?" He looked down at her with concern.

She shook her head.

"Just tell me," he said.

"I can't leave the boat. The marina is threatening to throw me out."

"Why would they do that? Joe's been at this dock for ages."

"The fees are overdue."

"Damn it, Dawn, why didn't you call me?"

"Call you?"

"Sure. There's some money put aside to help you maintain the boat."

There's no way in hell he mentioned that when she'd met with him. She sensed a lie. "You said all the money went to Joe's son."

He bobbled his head side to side. "It's complicated," he said. "But look, I'm dead serious about this. You need to get away. I'll take care of the fees."

She toed the dock. She hated handouts and yet, she'd been praying for something like this for days. "I don't have anywhere to go."

"Surely you have someone."

"I don't," she said, head down.

"Family?"

"Nope."

"Friends?"

She shifted uncomfortably on her feet and shook her head, hair falling into her eyes. She pushed it away. "No."

"All right then, take the Papa Joe off shore for a few days."

"I can't leave. The marina will—"

"I told you I'd take care of the fees. When you come back, your slip will still be here."

She bit her lip. What she really wanted was to be at the courthouse in case Felix and his henchman Orly showed up.

And Dylan. A ball of fire burned in her gut at the thought of him. She'd sworn to him that she would find him again.

But that was after he'd sworn to find her to even the score. She might be down on her luck, but she didn't have a death wish.

"Will you go?"

She didn't see how she could. No money for food or diesel, but she kept her mouth shut about that. One handout per morning was all her pride could stomach.

"I will. When's the hearing?"

"Friday. I recommend you be gone well before then." His eyes slid to his wrist again. "I have to go. Promise me you'll be away."

"I will."

"Good." He turned on his heel to go.

"Wait," she said. "When will the trial be?"

"That's what the hearing's for," he said. "I'll be in touch on that. Next time, answer your damn phone." He turned his back to her and she watched him walk away with long, elegant strides. He must have been a real lady's man when he was younger.

"Wait," she said again. He turned back, a hint of impatience flashed over his fine features. "Thank you for coming down here."

The corner of his mouth quirked, he tipped his chin, then turned and hurried up the dock.

CHAPTER FIFTEEN

As Dawn measured generous spoonfuls of coffee into the percolator, she heard a click outside as the shore power was restored. The lawyer worked fast, she was impressed. She still thought his story was bullshit. If there'd been money, he would have said so when he read the will. But with her back against the wall, she was grateful to have the fees paid. She'd pay him back later. She lit the burner and took a quick inventory of the cupboards while she waited for her caffeine fix.

Two cans of tomatoes, a box of spaghetti, some rice of unknown origin and age, and a tin of sardines in mustard sauce so old she could barely read the label. Perhaps not the most appetizing collection but she could stretch the spaghetti for at least a couple of days and sardines had plenty of protein. Or so she'd heard. She hated sardines.

In the wheelhouse, she turned the key and watched the gas gauge climb to just over a quarter tank. Pretty much the same as the last time she'd checked. She wouldn't go far on that. Or-- as Joe used to say--she could go far, she just wouldn't make it back.

She splashed hot coffee into her favorite mug and pored

over a couple charts in the wheelhouse, looking for a nearby hidey hole to hunker down in for a few days. She made a mental note of a couple of coves where she and Joe had done some fishing. It was possible tourists could stumble across her there, but mostly she'd be in calm waters. If she left under cover, at night, nobody would even know in which direction to start looking.

Back in the galley, she pulled down the coffee can with her cash stash and said a silent thank you to Shorty. She emptied it out on the table, making little piles of bills and coins. Very little piles. There was much less than she'd thought. She wouldn't go far on this money.

The urgency of the lawyer's words came back to her. She'd be a sitting duck if she was here on the boat.

It surprised her again to realize that she didn't have a death wish. That in the bottom of her soul was a small flicker of self-preservation. Granted, it was fueled by vengeance. She planned to be around long enough to testify at the trial and put Joe's murderers behind bars.

She took another sip of coffee, gazing out the starboard window toward the open sea, until her thoughts were interrupted by a man's voice calling her name from the dock.

A whiny man's voice.

A man she'd done everything in her power to avoid.

Her eyes slid to the tin of sardines on the counter and back to the small pile of money before her on the table. She couldn't believe she was now going to have to deal with him. For at least an entire day. Maybe for more than a day. Her skin crawled like a palmetto beetle had sauntered across her.

Stepping into the sunshine, Dawn shielded her eyes, and forced a smile. "Good morning, Timothy."

When there was nowhere to go but down, you reached for the only straw that might save you.

CHAPTER SIXTEEN

"Just stack those boxes on the table in the galley." Standing on the back deck like the king of the world, Timothy barked out orders to a couple of scrawny delivery boys from the local grocery. With the elder of the two passing boxes up from the cart on the dock, and the other running the boxes into the galley, the two boys managed to get the job done in under five minutes.

When they were done, they remained beside their empty cart, hands stuffed in their pockets and staring up at Timothy. He didn't flinch. Man was duller than a turkey bone. Or just mean. Dawn wasn't sure which. She moved out onto the port side. "Good work boys," she said. She dug in her pocket and passed them a five. The elder of the two reached up for it, and they jogged back up the dock, the cart bumping rhythmically over the boards as they went.

Dawn had never seen so much food on the Papa Joe. The supplies Joe normally carried consisted of deli ham, cheese slices and a loaf of white bread. Chips, pretzels, Ritz crackers and some cheese. Maybe a bag of Oreos or Snickerdoodles thrown in for good measure.

"Who's gonna cook all this?" she asked, waving her hand at the boxes.

"That's the beauty of it," Timothy said. "It's all part of the course. They will."

"Well, let's get it stowed away before they arrive." She took the steps into the wheelhouse, leaving Timothy to deal with the food.

The charts with their course lay open on the chart table. She had another look over their route. They'd be gone three days and she'd managed to convince Timothy that the secluded coves were the best way to show the students how private and exclusive cruising could be.

"Hi ho," came a voice from the dock. Her eyes slid to the clock on the wall. Almost an hour early. Timothy stuck his head out the galley door.

"Good morning," he called, his tone pleasant. Timothy had surpassed her expectations, yet again, when he'd shown up this morning showered, cleanly shaven and sporting clean, fairly new clothes. He'd even had his hair cut. She had to admit he cleaned up pretty well. He'd promised her he'd do ninety percent of the interacting with their so-called students and she could focus on piloting the boat.

She took a quick peek through the wheelhouse window. A couple, she guessed them to be in their early seventies, stood on the dock, the man's arm looped casually over the woman's shoulder, with a porter behind them carrying two large suitcases.

The woman wore a scarlet red hat, suitable for the Kentucky Derby, and a flowing white dress, complete with a lace jacket. Her husband sported a linen suit and white canvas docksiders. They looked for all the world like they were ready to board First Class on the Titanic and reminded her of the rich couple from Gilligan's Island. She dubbed them the Howells, confident a sense of humor was likely the only way she'd make it through this trip.

Timothy stepped down onto the dock and shook the man's hand while introductions were made. When Timothy reached out to shake the wife's hand, she actually offered up the back of her hand to be kissed. Timothy, determined to ingratiate himself, bent his head and lightly brushed her skin with his lips.

"Welcome folks," he said. "This your luggage?"

"Just a few items for the weekend," Mrs. Howe said.

From his back pocket, Timothy pulled a folded sheet of green paper and opened it. "I'm afraid we won't have room for that," he said. He ran his finger down the page and turned it so the couple could read it. "I have to insist on this luggage requirement. One small soft-sided bag each."

"Winston," she said, batting her lashes up at her husband, "surely *we're* not to be subjected to that silly rule."

"Now see here, my good man" Mr. Howe said, "we came early so you could get us situated before," he gave Timothy an exaggerated wink as he pulled his wallet out of his pocket, dug into the bills, and extended a crisp hundred-dollar bill, "before the other students arrive."

Timothy looked at the bill. Dawn could tell he was tempted. They were both in this for the money after all. But with six passengers plus themselves, they were full up.

He shook his head. "I'm sorry, Mr. Howe, there's nothing I can do. If you didn't bring soft-sided bags, I have a couple of duffel bags inside you can use to transfer some of your belongings."

Mrs. Howe wrung her hands and looked up at her husband, pleading, lashes still fluttering. "Winston."

"We can't be expected to unpack on the dock," the man huffed.

"I can take you up to the marina, there's an events room there where you can rearrange your luggage. But I'm afraid," Timothy looked back over his shoulder as he climbed on deck to retrieve the duffel bags, "I do have to insist that you only fill the duffels halfway and send the rest of your belongings back with your... " He looked down at the man helping them, clearly at a loss for words on what to call him. "Send the rest of your belongings home."

Dawn ducked her head quickly back into the wheelhouse as Mr. Howe edged backward to take a look at the boat. She hadn't been seen and didn't intend to be. Besides, considering they seemed to have been anticipating dinner at the Captain's table or dancing on the Lido deck, she expected he'd find the Papa Joe wanting.

She heard Timothy jump onto the dock and move away with them toward shore. Glad she didn't have to deal with them herself, she checked the time--another forty-five minutes--and returned her attention to the charts.

CHAPTER SEVENTEEN

THE THING ABOUT SETTING OUT TO SEA ON A BEAUTIFUL SUNNY day, with clear skies and a gentle undulating swell, is that everything seems possible. You leave the busy-ness of the city behind. Whatever the stresses of your day-to-day life, you shrug them off minutes after the boat pulls away from the pier. You focus in on the cries of the gulls overhead, the lap of the water against the bow, the steady drone and vibrations of the diesel beneath your feet.

Blah blah blah. Would Timothy ever shut up? Dawn kept her eye on the horizon, her landmark, and the compass and did her best to tune him out.

He'd started by getting everyone aboard, assigning bunks, and helping them stow their gear. They were a motley crew.

The Howes would sleep in the galley. It was the only bed suitable for a couple and they had a few years on the rest of the passengers. Mrs. Howe hadn't been happy to find she'd have to pass through the wheelhouse and climb down a set of stairs to get to the head--or *privy* as she'd called it--and Mr. Howe had suggested they take the forward cabin and the other three bunk elsewhere. Displaying a finesse Dawn didn't know he had in him, Timothy had handled each hiccup like a true politician. Whoever his ex-partner had been, she'd been a good influence.

With each small hurdle, Dawn's confidence in Timothy and them actually pulling off the course he'd been hired to give, increased. Maybe it wouldn't be so bad after all.

One of the forward berths was assigned to Jenny, a tall, lithe model with hair the color of copper and legs up to her arm pits. Her tangerine short shorts and nautical striped tank top lay against perfectly tanned skin. Dawn figured her for early twenties. So far, everything that had come out of her mouth simply confirmed Dawn's impression that she was an air head.

A little heavier built, with wavy dark hair, and an easy smile, the third female passenger's name was Megan. She was warm and bubbly and Dawn liked her on sight. She wore proper deck shoes with her hair clipped back to stay out of her eyes. She'd also sleep forward.

A third forward berth would go to Erik. Dawn had dubbed him the Professor on sight. He'd turned up as she was firing up the diesel and asked a zillion questions. He wanted to know about everything. She half expected him to repeat it all into a recording app or take notes. Despite his enthusiasm, which grated on her--she didn't enjoy so much interaction or attention--he had an easy manner and was a quick learner. He'd probably be helpful to have around. He insisted on calling her Captain D, it caught on quickly and the others followed suit.

After waiting almost an hour for the sixth passenger, Timothy had recommended they get under sail. No sense in penalizing those who had shown up on time and besides, he told her, his course preparation material had been very specific about the boat not waiting for latecomers.

As long as she got paid, Dawn had no qualms with that argument. After narrating everything she did in preparation to leave the dock, Timothy had shown Megan and Erik how to cast off the lines and put Jenny in charge of stowing the bumpers.

The Howes were in the kitchen chopping vegetables for a salad. Shoulder to shoulder in the small space, they laughed like school children. She supposed it was a lark for them to be doing such menial work. It was easy to picture them in a large estate with full-time cooks and housekeepers and sitting at opposite ends of a long table, eating duck a l'orange with watercress salad, and discussing the latest charity Mrs. Howe was involved with.

Timothy continued to wax poetic about the thrill of being at sea, until Erik interrupted him to ask about the electrical system on board the Papa Joe. Timothy shot her a look and outlined the basics of onboard power. She tipped her chin.

"The Papa Joe has a pretty standard set up," Dawn said. They all focused their attention on her. "However, Joe, the previous owner and namesake of the boat, also installed a solar power system on the top deck. We haven't used it much, but it's in place in case we need it."

"What if the sun doesn't shine?" Jenny asked.

"Do I detect a New York accent?" Erik asked her.

"Born upstate," she said, "but now I live in New York. The city," she rushed on to add.

Megan stifled a small smile, but also seemed a bit intimidated by her. Dawn got that. Jenny practically looked airbrushed.

"Right," Erik said. "I thought so. The thing is, in Florida, we mostly have sunny days."

"Except when we have hurricanes," Megan said.

"Hurricanes?" Mrs. Howe's voice floated up from the galley. "I thought Timothy said the weather is clear for the next three days."

"It is Mrs. Howe." Timothy stepped to the top of the galley

steps. "Erik is just giving Jenny a lesson in Florida weather." Mrs. Howe twittered.

"Now, good sir," Mr. Howe said, the humor rich in his voice, "I saw that wink. You're not flirting with my lovely bride, are you?" Mrs. Howe's laughter tinkled behind him.

"How are you getting along with the lunch prep?" Timothy descended into the galley and Dawn was left with the other three.

"Have you lived here long?" Jenny asked Megan. Megan responded but Dawn didn't hear her answer as Erik inserted himself between her and Megan's back.

"You look at home behind the wheel," he said. "How long have you had your boat?"

It was a question Dawn hadn't anticipated. Her brow creased, and she quickly opted for vague. "A while now."

"Converted Cape Cod?"

Dawn's esteem for Erik raised a couple of notches. "It is. Belonged to a good friend before I inherited it."

"She's beautiful," Erik said. "I've always preferred wooden boats to fiberglass."

"They each have their advantages," she said, thinking of the hours she and Joe had spent in the dry dock painting the hull. Her neck had hurt for days and she'd picked red paint flakes out of her hair for even longer

"And you've kept her old school," he said.

She raised her brow in question.

"No electronics." He waved a hand. "No radar, fish finder, that sort of thing."

"More the previous owner's choice than mine," she said. "I'll probably upgrade but for now I just use an App."

"There's an app for that?" He laughed.

She laughed back and he leaned in close to her, too close. She stepped slightly to the right and said, "Maybe you'd like to take the helm for a bit."

"Really?" His eyes brightened.

"Why not?" She set him up behind the wheel and indicated an island to the south east. "Head for that point," she said. "You can't go wrong."

"Wait," he said, as she started to move away, "I had a couple more questions."

"Plenty of time later," she said. "I have a few other things to take care of. You'll do fine." She waved off the rest of his concerns and hustled out the starboard door of the wheelhouse, down the side and scooted up the ladder onto the top deck. Under the bright sun, she lowered herself as quietly as she could over the window of the wheelhouse, where she'd always sat to talk with Joe when he was at the wheel.

Too many people, too much chatter. And yet, as she watched the gulls soaring above, she found she was starting to appreciate some of what Timothy had been saying earlier. She was leaving the stress of her day-to-day behind her. She realized she was even feeling optimistic about this course, this trip, this opportunity to make some money.

More importantly, as far as she could tell, nobody had seen them leave the harbor, nobody knew where they were going, and by nightfall they'd be secreted away in a little-known cove, tucked in and safe for the night.

CHAPTER EIGHTEEN

THE SEAGULLS DAWN WAS WATCHING FLOCKED OVER TO circle a fishing boat coming back in from a morning haul. The boat steamed straight toward them and she popped her head down over the side so she could speak to Erik through the window.

"You see that boat heading toward us?"

"I do," he said, maintaining his heading.

"You might want to move the wheel slightly, just to the eleven o'clock position," she said.

"Won't that take us off our heading?"

She brushed the hair out of her eyes, feeling the blood rushing into her head. "A bit. We'll correct later. Once the boat passes us."

"You got it, Captain D," he said, giving her a half salute.

"What are you doing up here?" Timothy's stage whisper behind her brought her head up out of the wheelhouse. She turned to look at him.

"Getting a little sun," she said.

"You left a brand new student on the wheel?" He crossed his arms and widened his stance, glaring down at her.

"It's not rocket science," she said. "Besides, I'm right here."

He stepped closer and dropped his voice even lower. "Sure, but being on the wheel should come on the last day, not at the very beginning."

She shrugged. "What difference does it make?"

"The difference," he said, "is we're not selling the steak, we're selling the sizzle."

"What?" She shook her head.

"What I mean is, we need to spin things so there's a little more mystery and build their skills slowly. Once they have a foundation of the basics, then they can move on to more important things."

"Like being on the wheel?" She chuckled and resisted rolling her eyes when his pupils darkened.

He crouched down at her side. "We're selling a course. We need to be able to teach them something. Most of it is showmanship, and making sure they all get along."

"I realize you have some sort of curriculum," she said, "but I think you're making too big a deal out of this."

"Oh, you think that I am. Well, aye aye Captain. I forgot which one of us had the experience with this." His mouth twisted as his eyes became hard.

"Don't be rude, Timothy," she said. "I'm not supposed to have to deal with the students at all. That's what you promised."

"I was busy in the galley. Surely it won't kill you to chat them up for a few minutes."

"Keep your voice down," she said. "Everything we say up here can be heard below."

"Yes, well... " Timothy stared out over the water toward the gulls, his face flushed.

Dawn knew that look, she'd seen it lots in the gym. Defeated but not willing to admit it took a lot out of a person. Nobody liked to lose face. "Look, it's not a big deal. Let's just figure out what's next. For what it's worth, I think it's going great so far."

"You do?" Timothy's shoulders straightened as he searched her eyes.

"I do. So what's next?"

"The Howes will have lunch ready soon. Then we'll clean up. After lunch, I'll teach them some navigation skills. But you need to let me decide how quickly they learn."

She shrugged and stared off into the sky. "Sure."

"Really," he pressed. "Just let me take care of it."

"Then *take* care of it," she said, meeting his gaze. "Don't leave me to entertain them."

"I'm sure they weren't that entertained." Timothy stood and stalked across the deck to the ladder. A few seconds later his voice drifted up from below.

She scrambled down the ladder and back inside, relieving Erik. "You go ahead and pay attention to Timothy," she said, easing back into her place behind the wheel.

"Thanks, Dawn," Timothy said, in a pleasant tone. "So we have everything stowed away, we've set a course, and we're well underway out of the harbor. Mr. And Mrs. Howe, can you come up here for a minute please?" A moment later, after some clattering of utensils and cookware, the couple joined them in the wheelhouse.

"How's lunch coming along?"

"We just need a few more minutes and it'll be ready," Mrs. Howe said.

"Great, thanks. Lunch is free time. You can find a spot in the galley or out aft, or on the forward deck, wherever you feel comfortable eating. Once lunch is done, Jenny and Megan you'll be on clean up duty." The two women nodded their agreement.

"After lunch, we'll come back to the wheelhouse and spend most of the afternoon learning how to read a chart, use the compass and set a course. Sound good?"

Following a chorus of yeses, Mr. And Mrs. Howe returned to the galley. A moment later, Mr. Howe called up that lunch was ready.

"If it's ready, let's go eat," Timothy said, shepherding the students toward the stairs. He glanced back at Dawn and lifted a brow. She raised her hands in a silent applause and let out a breath as he followed the students to lunch, leaving her alone with her thoughts.

CHAPTER NINETEEN

THE CHEERFUL SOUNDS OF PEOPLE CHATTING OVER A MEAL floated up to Dawn. By the sound of it, most of the students had stayed in the galley. Technically there was room for four adults at the table, but you could squeeze in five if you were determined. Erik had taken his plate up to the bow and sat, back ramrod straight, on top of the forward cabin, picking at his food and gazing out to sea.

Once the students had been served, Timothy loaded up a plate and brought it up to Dawn, setting it on the console beside her without a word. Despite his offer--and assurances--it seemed that being First Mate to a novice Captain, let alone a woman, was not sitting that well with him. He'd have to get over that. From Dawn's point of view, she'd saved his feet from the fire as much as he'd saved hers. Without her boat and her time, he'd have to cancel the course and forfeit all the course money. With his boat stuck at the pier, like a duck with a lame wing, he couldn't afford to do that.

Her eyes followed a splash of motion to the far north. She picked up the binoculars and followed a speedboat racing over the top of the waves. It was too far out to make out the type of boat or number of passengers, but her stomach clenched. Since Joe's lawyer had shown up yesterday morning, she'd been on edge. Each creak of the dock, each unrecognized face, and now, apparently, each speedboat on the horizon caused her a measure of concern. At this rate, she'd have an ulcer before she hit thirty.

The day would come when she'd find Dylan again, the man who'd been responsible for all the trouble on the Papa Joe. She rubbed her wrist. At times, the break still pulsed like some foreign being trying to escape beneath her skin. The dull crack of the bone under Dylan's weight was as fresh to her today as when it had happened.

Plus Felix and his miserable little henchman Orly. Those two jokers were right behind Dylan on her hit list. Thugs, criminals, opportunists. Murderers. She planned to be good and ready when she saw those three losers again. And it wouldn't be while she was on a cruise with five clueless passengers and Gilligan.

The helplessness she'd felt that day blind-sided by Dylan and his crew, Nico and Mark, still stung. She wished again she could be there for the hearing. She itched to *do* something instead of just waiting around.

The boat was closing the distance between them, the waves splashing around the bow now clear. She picked up the binoculars again and took a look. A young couple with a small child in the back. A few minutes later, they turned to the east and cut across her bow a quarter of a mile out. The tightness in her chest eased.

If she ever got her hands on Dylan again, she'd kill him. The fury that whipped through her made her hands tremble on the wheel. He'd taken so much from her that she couldn't even... couldn't even breathe. Her fingers clenched the smooth wood of the wheel as she tried to ground herself, gulping in air. In her mind's eye, she watched the ginger-haired bastard lift Joe and hurl him over the side of the boat.

The stuff of her nightmares. Joe sailing through the air, hands bound tightly behind him, his body sinking beneath the surface as Dylan laughed in her face. She'd find the Irish bastard and, when she did, he'd no longer be laughing.

"Not eating, hon?" Mrs. Howe stood beside her, pointing at the plate of food Dawn had ignored.

Dawn tried to shake off the memory. "It looks delicious," she said. "I was just waiting for a drink."

Mrs. Howe reached out and placed her hand on Dawn's forearm. "I can get you a drink, dear." Before Dawn could protest she turned away and went back into the galley.

She needed to pull herself together. The speedboat was a family out for a joy ride on a beautiful Thursday afternoon. Her boat was full of students, who, she reluctantly had to admit, seemed like good enough people. At least so far there was nobody she wanted to kill. Except Timothy.

Picking up the fork, she speared an olive and popped it in her mouth. Even Timothy had dialed down his annoyance factor on her tolerance meter. He wasn't perfect, far from it, but without him, without this course and the money it would bring in, and the perfect opportunity to get out of town for a few days, she'd be sitting on the Papa Joe at the marina waiting for possible disaster.

Mrs. Howe appeared with a glass of sweet tea, the condensation already beading the glass. She thanked her, took a long pull of the cool liquid, and nodded in appreciation. The woman smiled, her plump face sporting dimples where they weren't intended, then turned to enjoy the view of the island they were approaching.

No, Dawn had to admit that so far things were going more smoothly than she could have imagined.

However, they'd only been aboard a few hours and there were many more hours to go.

CHAPTER TWENTY

As the sun started inching toward the westward horizon, Timothy finally wrapped up the navigation portion of his course. For the most part things went well, and Dawn, unable to totally tune things out, had even picked up a couple of tips herself. Not that she ever intended to reveal that to him.

The students had followed Timothy's words closely, asking intelligent questions--Erik more than all of them combined--and Timothy was clearly in his element. She would never have imagined him a good teacher, but they seemed to love him and he had a way of explaining concepts that made them easy to grasp.

Mrs. Howe and Megan had some trouble working out how to calculate a heading using the compass. Midway through their questions, Erik jumped in only convoluting things even more. The two women became increasingly flustered as Erik repeatedly drew the same diagram on a sheet of paper.

Dawn itched to interrupt. Joe had taught her a very simple system for the compass and each word out of Erik's mouth made things seem more and more complicated. However, after the incident with the wheel earlier, she didn't want to step on Timothy's toes. She'd let him handle it.

Timothy did eventually jump in and take control back from Erik. He seemed intimidated by Erik's obvious years of higher education which he wore like a badge, often deferring to him when it wasn't necessary.

The session with the charts went better, with everyone huddled around Timothy as he traced the rest of their course for the day and pointed out their anchorage for the night.

"And tomorrow?" Jenny asked, as Timothy stepped back from the chart table.

"Tomorrow you'll have a chance to plot the course yourself." He smiled at her warmly, his eyes flashed to her cleavage, then back to her face.

The corner of Jenny's mouth twitched and over Timothy's shoulder, she caught Dawn's eye.

Timothy clapped his hands. "That's it for now," he said. "Free time. You can spend some time on deck and enjoy the fresh air while we cruise to our destination for the night. Be sure to watch for some of the landmarks you saw on the charts as we go by," he reminded them as they filed out of the cabin.

"Good job reigning in the Professor," Dawn said.

He shot her a look. "I did the best I could."

She held up her palm. "I wasn't being sarcastic. I thought you did a good job in a difficult situation."

Timothy's eyes widened slightly and his shoulders dropped. He clearly expected trouble from her, but she was learning quickly that he responded much better to praise than criticism. "Um, thanks."

For a Thursday afternoon, there were a lot of boats in the channel and it was making her nervous. Her whole plan had been to get to their chosen spot for the night unseen. "I've been thinking it might be a good idea to anchor behind this next island. Should be able to find a place in the lee to stop for a bit"

"Why would we want to do that? I thought we already agreed on a stop for the night?"

"Not for the night. Maybe a swim and rest a little before we head to the cove."

"If you need a rest, I can take the wheel for a while," Timothy said. "Sorry I didn't consider it before. I'm sure you could use a break."

That's an angle she hadn't seen coming. "It's a beautiful day for a swim," she said. "Why don't we just stop for a bit?"

He slanted a look at her. "I really think it's best we just carry on and get settled for the night." He reached toward his back pocket.

She dismissed the paper he pulled out. "I don't need to see the curriculum," she said. "We're only forty-five minutes away from our spot for the night. Plus, I was realizing watching the sun that the orientation is going to be wrong later for the sunset. Wouldn't it be more atmospheric for us to have dinner here, watching the sunset, and then carry on?"

Timothy opened his mouth, but Dawn cut him off. She had no intention of cruising into their hidden cove with so much activity around them.

"Seriously, think of the photographs they'll take. The memories of their first night on the boat. Could be good for future business."

"You want to do this again?" Timothy's face brightened.

"I meant for you."

"Oh. Well, I still think it will be hard to explain why we're stopping."

"Hard to explain that it's a good spot for a swim? That we want to see the sunset? You can sell it. It's one of the perks of having your own boat, right? Being able to take advantage of opportunities as they arise. Being spontaneous and open to the world. You know, where everything seems possible." She echoed his words from his opening speech back to him.

Timothy painstakingly folded the paper in his hand and tucked it back into his pocket. "Well, you're the Captain," he said finally. "If you want me to sell it, I will. But the whole point was to teach the course the way I know how to do it." He turned to leave.

Relieved, Dawn let out a sigh.

Timothy turned back, his brows raised. "Why were you fighting so hard for this? Is there something you're not telling me?"

Surprised at his keen observation, Dawn silently kicked herself. He'd been so close to letting it slide. "I just think we should enjoy the time we have out here."

"That's all?" His eyes narrowed. "Why did you decide to do this trip? For someone so dead set against it, you sure change your mind quickly."

Dawn's gut clenched. This was going in a really bad direction. She cast her eyes to her feet and lowered her voice. "You know why. Same reason as you. Money." She raised her head and met his stare. He wasn't backing down.

She tried a different approach. "Come on, let's stop, have a swim, show these folks how much fun being on the water can be. Also, it's a great teaching moment."

"How so?"

"Two opportunities to practice with the anchor." She turned the wheel slowly as they cleared the southern tip of the island. As she'd expected, beyond the point, there was flat water. She tilted her chin, indicating the spot to Timothy. "Look. Beautiful spot to swim and a clear view of the sunset later."

"Fine," he said, peevishly. "I'll go *sell it* and teach them how to set an anchor." He leaned in so close his warm breath brushed her cheek. "I still think there's more going on here than you're letting on. Just putting you on notice about that." He whirled and stomped away. Dawn watched him go, forcing a breath through her nose before she refocused on the task at hand.

Dawn steered the boat around the end of the point toward the lee side of the island. On the bow, everyone gathered for the impromptu lesson. There was a lot of gesturing to the line, to the anchor, and heads turned repeatedly between her and the bow and the anchor. At one point, Megan stuck her finger in her mouth, then pulled it out and held it up to test the wind. Dawn chuckled. In turn they each tested the weight of the anchor. She throttled down and idled into the current. Mr. Howe stepped up to the side with the anchor.

There was a large splash. On the bow, Mr. Howe still held the anchor. Dawn's brain struggled to catch up with her ears. The splash hadn't been the anchor. She yelled out the window. "What was that?"

Eyes wide as platters, Timothy's head swiveled while he counted his students.

CHAPTER TWENTY-ONE

"MAN OVERBOARD," YELLED TIMOTHY.

Dawn shut down the engine, calculating how long it would take for the prop to stop spinning. Pandemonium broke out on the bow as everyone started screaming Jenny's name and trying to move at once.

"Be quiet," Timothy yelled. "And stay still. Panic isn't going to help. Erik, you come with me." Dawn watched as they made their way toward the stern. As he passed the window, he said, "It's Jenny."

Megan ran behind them. "Jenny can't swim."

What the hell? There was someone on board who couldn't swim and hadn't been wearing a life jacket? She sprinted to the aft deck through the galley. "Timothy, can you see her?"

"I see where she went in," said Erik, already lifting his T-shirt over his head. Before she or Timothy could stop him, he dove into the water and swam toward a blister of air bubbles with long, strong strokes.

Timothy grabbed the life preserver from the wall, ready to throw it out. Dawn reached for a boat hook, motioned Megan close and passed it to her.

"I need to get an anchor in," Dawn said. The current was quickly pushing them backward toward the spot where Jenny went under. A small rip tide would quickly carry the Papa Joe onto the rocks at the point. She knew there wasn't much depth within a hundred feet of the rocks.

Racing to the bow, she found Mr. Howe lowering the anchor carefully to the deck. "Give it to me," she said. Stunned, he held it out to her like it was a large pile of freshly laundered towels. She threw it into the water, ran the line between her hands, hoping it would catch as the current continued to push them backwards.

She calculated the distance between the stern and the rocks. She had time, only barely, to start the engine again and get them out of danger of going aground, but she couldn't see what was going on behind the boat.

"Mrs. Howe, go find out what's going on and get back here as quickly as you can. Hurry!"

Dawn continued to let the line out, watching the shoreline behind them, the bow starting to swing to the port side with a gust of wind that came from nowhere.

A sudden tautness to the line running through her fingers told her the anchor had caught and she heaved out a breath. She turned to find Mr. Howe still standing behind her, mouth open. She cleated off the line then said, "Watch this line," she said. She pointed to a large tree on shore. "Keep your eye on that tree, and if we start to move, you call for me immediately."

"But—"

She was already gone, down the port side, so she wouldn't run into Mrs. Howe who she could see making her way back up along the starboard. As Dawn stepped onto the aft deck, Erik surfaced with Jenny. Timothy threw the life preserver and missed. He started reeling the line back in. Megan bounced in place at the stern, ready with the grappling stick.

Jenny was struggling, arms flailing as she tried to break free of Erik's grasp. Dawn dove into the water. Keeping them both in her view, she closed the distance between them. As she reached them, she heard the splash of the preserver off to their right. She reached for it and pushed it between herself and Jenny.

"Jenny, take this. Hang on!"

Seemingly unaware of Dawn's presence, Jenny pushed down on Erik's shoulders and he went under. When he surfaced, he spit up water.

"Push her away from you," Dawn yelled.

"I'm trying." Jenny's elbow smashed him across the nose. Dawn heard it crack.

"Push. Push her to the preserver." While she continued yelling at Erik, she nudged the preserver up against Jenny's body. She swiveled, lashed out, and then grabbed it. Now that she was above the surface, Dawn was able to get her attention. "Jenny, hang on to the preserver. You're going to be all right."

Behind Jenny, Erik held his hand to his face, blood spurted from his nose. "Jenny, just hang on. We're going to get you in. You're safe now."

Wide-eyed and hysterical, Jenny clawed at the preserver.

"Stay calm, Jenny," Dawn said, and gave Timothy the thumbs up to start pulling the preserver toward the boat. The only thing she knew to do now was keep talking. Timothy would have to do the rest from on board.

Together, she and Erik swam alongside Jenny, nearby but careful to stay out of her reach, as Timothy pulled her closer to the stern. As they got closer, Dawn swam ahead and pulled herself up onto the swimming platform.

"Timothy, come help me," she said. "Megan, you handle the line."

Megan dropped the hook and took over the line while Timothy stepped down onto the platform. Once Jenny was below them, they reached under her arms and lifted her up, spewing and coughing, onto the platform. Her eyes rolled in her head like a deranged doll.

With no room for Erik on the platform, Dawn climbed back on deck to get out of the way. Erik pulled himself out of the water, breathing heavily, nose bleeding freely, and leaned back against the flat of the stern.

Timothy leaned Jenny forward and pounded on her back. She coughed up a bucket of seawater, followed by lunch. Her beautiful face blanched bone white, her lips tight, then she slumped against Timothy's shoulder, exhausted.

"Megan, grab a clean dish towel and the first aid kit," Dawn said. "It's in the galley. Over the sink."

Megan pulled the life preserver up onto the deck then spun around into the galley. She was back in seconds and passed both to Dawn.

"Here Erik," Dawn said, passing the towel down to him. He shoved it up to his nose to staunch the bleeding, wiped at his mouth with his other hand, then spat into the water.

"You feeling well enough to climb back up here?" she asked him.

He nodded and pulled himself to a standing position. "She fought like a banshee," he said.

"Drowning people usually do," Dawn said, extending her hand to guide him to the ladder.

Once he was on deck, she turned her attention to Timothy and Jenny. "How is she? Let me get down there so we can bring her back up."

Timothy looked up at her, and his mouth dropped.

"Jaysus, Dawn," he said. She followed his gaze, cursed loudly, and sprang into action.

CHAPTER TWENTY-TWO

Dawn raced through the cabin to the wheelhouse and pushed the ignition. Her heart pounded. They were drifting backward toward the rocks, the anchor dragging along the bottom.

She yelled for Megan. Seconds later, she was in the wheelhouse. "Go up on the bow and have Mr. Howe help you bring the anchor in. If you can't get it all the way up, just hold it off the side of the bow. In fact, do it that way. Just hold it off the side, cause we'll need to drop anchor again."

Dawn yelled again. "Timothy?"

"All clear," he yelled back.

Mr. Howe sat on the forward cabin chatting with his wife, like they were enjoying a Sunday brunch. He wasn't even facing toward the shore and the tree she had asked him to keep an eye on. He remained blissfully unaware, despite the frantic activity and yelling, that anything was wrong. Why was he even on this course if he planned to fall back on his wealth and mis-guided sense of privilege?

Megan cast a look over her shoulder and decided to pull the

anchor in on her own. Dawn stuck her head out the window. "He can help you."

"It's not heavy, I'm fine, I've done this before."

Dawn eased forward on the throttle, bringing the bow up over the anchor, and Megan pulled it in, hand over hand, the line coiling on the deck in loose loops . As instructed, she held it steady just above the surface, careful not to let it hit the hull.

A rip pulled the bow forward and Megan braced herself. Dawn leaned out the starboard door as far as possible to keep an eye on the point behind her.

"Timothy, I need your eyes. How close are we to those rocks?"

"Forward," he yelled as he hurried up the side toward her. "We're maybe fifty feet away from the rocks. According to the chart, there's almost no draw here. We could go aground."

"I'm aware of that," Dawn said, her jaw clenched. She pushed the throttle forward, giving the boat more power. The bow sliced through the calm water.

Megan put her hand up. "Wait. I can see bottom."

Dawn throttled back, put the boat in Neutral. "How deep?"

"I can't tell exactly." She cocked her head to the side, apologetically.

"Timothy, get the hell up there," Dawn said, but Timothy was already moving and she was talking to his back.

"We have about four feet here," he called back. Dawn's heart sank as a soft sliding sound came from beneath the hull as the rudder moved through sand. If she didn't correct things, the soft sliding sound could soon become a gravely scraping sound. Soon after that, they'd be aground.

"We're grounding out back here." Erik's voice came from the back galley door. "What can I do to help?"

"Just keep your eyes open. How far are we from the rocks?"

"Thirty feet," he said.

Thirty feet? They'd been fifty feet before she started moving forward.

"Thirty yards," he yelled. "I meant thirty yards."

So why were they grounding out? "Timothy, come take the wheel."

Timothy left Megan watching over the bow and was back at Dawn's side in seconds. She stepped away to the chart table. The soft sliding noise beneath them continued. She steeled herself for the grating.

She found their location and squinted at the chart, her nose almost touching the paper. Stepping back to the wheel, she took over the helm, put the boat in Forward and hit the throttle.

"Cripes, Dawn, do you know what you're doing?" Timothy tried to push her aside. She pushed back, edging the RPM higher. "You're going to run us aground," he said, trying again to shove her away from the controls. "Have you lost your mind?"

She shoulder checked him and he grunted and stumbled to the left a few inches.

The Papa Joe surged forward, a loud whooshing sound scraping along the bottom of the hull and then, silence. They were free. Gliding over the surface, unfettered. She kicked the throttle back and slanted a look at Timothy. "Sandbar."

"Good call, Captain," he said, with more than a trace of admiration in his voice. He rubbed his shoulder. "Sorry about… all that."

"Don't let it happen again," she said, her voice dead calm. "My boat, my call."

She piloted the boat forward for several more minutes until she was comfortable they were far enough away from the rocks and the sandbar. As before, she picked a nice spot in the lee that would afford them an excellent view of the sunset. Her feet felt grounded on the deck, her decisions sure, her place at the helm of her boat cemented.

"You want to give Megan a hand with that anchor?" she asked Timothy. "And right after that, once we have Jenny and Erik settled, I'm adding a little something to the *curriculum*, under the category of life jackets."

CHAPTER TWENTY-THREE

THE AFTERNOON SHIFTED INTO EVENING ALMOST UNNOTICED as time stretched imperceptibly in that lazy afternoon way. Beneath the boat, crystal waters shimmered over a rippled sandy bottom. Heat beat down on them from the vivid May sun. It was the perfect day for a swim and a sunset.

Except nobody felt like swimming after the misadventure they'd had.

On the aft deck, Megan hovered over Jenny. She'd wrapped her in a thick sleeping bag and propped her up in a deck chair Timothy had set up. Jenny was pale, but at least she'd stopped shaking.

"You had quite a scare," Dawn said, perching on the gunwale beside her. "Brave of you to be on a boat when you can't swim." She didn't intend the statement to be a judgement but from the look on Jenny's face, she'd interpreted it that way.

Dawn reached out and laid her hand on the woman's slender wrist. "I'm glad you're okay. We were all frightened."

Jenny nodded and let her gaze slip off to the side, back to the sunlight shifting over the turquoise waters.

On the bow, Timothy let out a whoop. "Got a good one," he yelled.

"What is that boy making so much fuss about?" Mr. Howe asked, beads of sweat covering his forehead. He looked like he would melt into a puddle at any moment in his linen suit.

"Why don't you and Mrs. Howe keep Timothy company up front?" Dawn suggested, still annoyed with him. "He's fishing for our supper and I'm sure he has an extra rod or two."

Mr. Howe wiggled his brows at his wife and off they went.

Jenny expelled a sigh as the crowd thinned out and she nodded gratefully at Dawn before turning her attention back to the water.

"How are you doing, Erik?" Dawn shifted her focus. Before she got in the ring professionally, she'd worked as an assistant to one of the cutman who worked out of Charlie's Gym. Plus, she'd picked up a trick or two from the way her own cut man had patched her up between rounds.

Erik, his head back, had his eyes closed. His nose was broken, squashed against his face and listing to one side, and there would be some bruising, the skin already yellowing, but it didn't look bad. She'd seen worse. Dried blood caked in a thin line above his upper lip, giving the appearance of poorly applied lipliner.

She grabbed a clean cloth from the stack Megan had assembled on the deck and dipped it into a bucket of water. "Do you mind?" she said, as she leaned forward to dab at his face.

He peeked out at her beneath a half-open lid. "Wet."

She chuckled. "Yeah, water normally is."

He jerked his head as she dabbed at a open slash on his cheek where Jenny had scratched him. "What's in that water?"

"It's salt water," Megan said. "I just put the bucket overboard."

"Good thinking," Dawn said. "The salt water will help clean the wounds."

"How many wounds are we talking about here?" Erik asked, his lip tilted upward.

"Enough for a hero, but not a tragic hero. How's that?" Dawn continued dabbing at his face, wiping the sweat from his forehead, then wrung the cloth overboard and dipped it back in the bucket before rubbing the dried blood from his lips.

He frowned at her and pursed his lips.

"Don't do that," she said. "Try to leave your mouth slack and keep it closed."

"Are you telling me—" His eyes twinkled.

"To shut up? No, simply to keep your mouth closed." When she was satisfied she had it all, she tossed the cloth into the pink water and pushed the bucket to a corner.

Erik's shoulders were a mass of red lines, like a circular road map had been etched into his skin. She touched his shoulder. "Mind if I have a look?"

He leaned forward. Ugly red welts covered his back. Jenny had fought hard. Dawn's eyes widened but as she opened her mouth to say something, Erik put his finger to his lips and slanted a look toward Jenny. A gentleman. He didn't want to embarrass her.

Dawn emptied the bucket overboard, filled it, grabbed another clean cloth and worked on Erik's back. "I have some antibiotic cream I'll apply later," she said. "For now, we'll let the salt water and the sun dry things out."

"Thanks," he said. "I was thinking I could use a drink."

"I'm pretty sure we all can," she said. "I'll be right back."

She made her way to the bow where Timothy had caught two large groupers. "Nice catch," she said, toeing the cooler they floundered in. "Maybe we should get supper started."

"Erik and Megan were on dinner duty." He shrugged. "I'll clean the fish and put it on the grill. Could you throw a salad together? Maybe with Megan's help?"

"Megan is busy with Jenny." She turned to the Howes.

"Folks, we need you to do double duty in the kitchen today. Can you put together another delicious salad?"

Mrs. Howe slipped her hand onto her husband's thigh. For a brief moment, Dawn thought they would refuse. But Mr. Howe rose, helped his wife up, and smiled broadly. "Of course you can count on us." They minced their way down the port deck and in through the wheelhouse door.

Dawn huffed out a breath. "Good grief." She shook her head at Timothy. "What a mess."

"A glitch," he said. "They'll bounce back quickly, you'll see."

She grabbed the cooler. "I can take care of cleaning these," she said. "We have a couple hours before sunset, so let's get some good food and a little wine in these folks to help them relax. Can you get everyone set up with drinks after you start the grill?"

With a nod, Timothy brought in his line and prepared the rod to be stowed. Then he moved away and she was left on her own, with her thoughts and two big gasping groupers.

CHAPTER TWENTY-FOUR

After a dinner of fresh fish, tossed salad and two bottles of wine, everyone stretched out, full and slightly buzzed, on the stern and top deck, to watch the sunset. Florida sunsets were spectacular and this one was no different. The sky blazed with a spectrum of colors while Jenny and Megan snapped photos with their phones.

Stepping up to the plate, the Howes volunteered for cleanup duty and excused themselves to go inside.

"Once the sun slips below the horizon, we'll set sail for our spot for the night," Dawn said.

Jenny cocked her head. "Won't it be dark?"

"No, we'll have about an hour of twilight and we're less than forty-five minutes from our destination. You remember the small cove Timothy showed you on the charts earlier?"

She nodded.

"It's very beautiful. Kind of a hidden treasure for only those in the know." Dawn smiled at her and Jenny's tight expression relaxed.

"It's nice here," Jenny said.

"This isn't a good spot for the night. Too open, too shallow."

She stood, stretching her arms overhead. "You can fold up the chairs and stow them below the deck." She tapped the deck with an open palm to show them where. The two women and Erik nodded at her.

With a tilt of his head, Timothy motioned Dawn toward the bow of the boat and walked away. She joined him there. "What's up?"

"I'm thinking we should just stay here for the night."

"Did you miss the part where I said it's too open and too shallow?" She took a breath, determined not to let him under her skin again. At least not today.

"It's getting late." He gestured toward the horizon.

"We have plenty of time," she said. "I want you on the anchor and ask Megan to make sure things are stowed aft."

"Which is it?"

"What?"

"The anchor or Megan?"

Refusing to let him push her buttons, she said, "First sort Megan out and then take care of the anchor." She turned away then pivoted back. "Actually, maybe get Erik to help Megan. I'll check on the Howes and get Jenny inside."

Five minutes later, with Timothy on the bow and Jenny secure on the bench behind her in the wheelhouse, Dawn fired up the diesel and rode the bow slowly up over the anchor. Once Timothy had it on board, she steered the boat in a large arc to the starboard, leaving plenty of room between them and the point, put the stern to the sun, and set the heading for the small cove.

With all in order, she slid her butt up onto the Captain's chair and relaxed. On the shelf beside her, her phone pinged. She ignored it and watched Timothy coil the bow line, and, avoiding her eye, make his way down the port side toward the stern.

Her phone pinged again. It could be Duncan. Knowing she

may not have a signal in the cove, she picked it up and checked the notifications on screen.

In order to follow the criminal charges against Dylan's men and coverage of Joe's death, Dawn had set up several Google alerts. The notification was a Google alert about an Instagram post from *ModelJenny*, hashtag *DramaAtSea*, along with their coordinates.

Crap. Swiveling in her chair, she turned to see Jenny tapping away on her phone.

"What are you doing?" She reacted without thought and only when Jenny's head snapped up, did she realize how sharp her tone had been.

"Putting up a photo about the course," she said.

Dawn bit her lip. "I need you to stop that right now."

"Why?"

Dawn struggled for a reasonable explanation. "It's like I said out back, the cove we're going to is only known by locals. I don't want the location known."

"Well, okay," Jenny said, her eyes narrowed, "but we're not at that location yet. I promised my followers a blow by blow of this course. Plus, it's not every day you almost die and live to tell about it."

"Timothy," Dawn yelled.

Jenny rushed on. "If you're worried about liability, don't. I won't sue you."

Oh crap, she could sue them. Sucker punch to the gut. She was speechless.

"I mean, I'll sign something if you want. My followers are lapping it up. You know what they say. There's no bad publicity."

"Timothy!"

Timothy poked his head through the starboard door. "What? What?"

Dawn pointed at Jenny and her phone, struggling for words,

not wanting to sound crazy. "Jenny is posting about our location and her near drowning."

"Oh." Timothy shrugged. "Good publicity, I guess."

"Unless..." Dawn's shoulders lifted as she put her hands palm up in the air, waiting for Timothy to follow her line of thinking.

"Well, it is good publicity for the cruise," Jenny said, petulantly. She poked her screen and a second later Dawn's phone pinged again.

"Perhaps Jenny would be more comfortable in the galley with the Howes," Dawn said pointedly, staring at Timothy.

Timothy's open expression closed in on itself and he extended a hand to Jenny. "Come on down and join the rest of the students," he said. "There's still a bit of wine left."

A couple of minutes later, he stepped back into the wheelhouse, and stood at her side, hands on his hips. "What are you thinking?" he hissed. "We *want* her to post about the course. It's great for business."

"Are you really that dense?" Dawn responded in a whisper. "Does the liability issue totally escape you? She could sue us."

Timothy's eyes widened as the penny dropped. "I had everyone sign waivers. I think those will cover us."

He was more prepared than she'd anticipated. "Can I see one?"

"They're all online, but I can bring one up for us to have a look at a little later tonight." He regarded her closely. "Better now?"

"I still don't want our location going out to the world," she said.

"Why not? What's the big secret?"

"It's dangerous."

"Dangerous?" He scoffed. "You think we'll be boarded by pirates, hoping to make off with our riches?"

She bit her tongue. She couldn't tell him. "Look, we're heading into some pretty secluded areas, places only the locals know about. Do you want to be responsible for opening those up to every Tom, Dick and Harriette with a pleasure craft? Even the tour operators don't take the tourists into those spots."

She watched him while he digested her lie. The best lie, she knew, always had an element of truth in it.

"That's true." He jammed his hands in his pockets. "I can ask them to only reveal our location while we're in open water."

"While you're at it, why not ask them to turn off the locations on their phones?" This was the only way she'd feel truly safe.

"What? I'm not sure I can take it that far."

"Why not? Make it... I don't know, seem like a treasure hunt or something."

He grunted. "I swear, I can't even begin to figure out what is going on in that head of yours. Frankly," he said, turning from her, "I'm not sure I want to know."

CHAPTER TWENTY-FIVE

CICADAS BUZZED ALONG THE SHORELINE AND A PAIR OF TERNS dipped and flirted along the still surface of the cove. Overhead, stars pulsed into view, one by one, and a ribbon of deep purple along the horizon was the only color left in the sky.

Dawn loved this time of day as the long day slipped into darkness. Even as a child, she'd loved the darkness. Her brother had often crept into her room at night when he'd had nightmares because she was always awake, always calm. Together they would snuggle and giggle into the night until one of their parents, usually their father, came in and issued an ultimatum. Go to sleep or be separated. They'd never pushed it to see if he would follow through.

On the stern, Timothy chatted with the Howes. Occasionally a snatch of their conversation drifted up to her. Megan and Jenny were in the wheelhouse and Erik somewhere below.

Mr. Howe stood up and yawned. "I think lovey and I will turn in for the night. Is it okay to close up the galley?"

"Sure," Timothy said, "let me grab a couple of items and show you how to get the bed down." The Howes followed

Timothy inside. After a few minutes, he stepped back outside and placed a large basket on the deck loaded with spirits, sodas, plastic cups, and a large bag of pretzels.

He disappeared inside and Dawn could hear him walking them through how to fold down the table and set up the bed. Neither of them asked a single question and she'd put money that the following night, and the night after that, Timothy would again be showing them how to set up the bed.

Once he was done, he closed the slider between the wheelhouse and galley, then Dawn heard light strains of Bob Marley pump through the PA as he turned on music. One of the Howes closed the door to the back of the galley cabin and their light chatter floated up to her through the open galley windows.

She was tempted to pull out her phone and try to reach Duncan to hear how the hearing had gone, but remembered the hearing was Friday and today was only Thursday. She chuckled. Being on the water really had, in part, helped her leave some of her worries behind.

"Mind if I join you?" Erik's head popped up over the deck.

She waved him up and he sat cross-legged across from her, facing the bow and the west horizon. He set a large bottle of sparkling water and two wine glasses between them. "Drink?"

"Sure." She looked at him through the last of the light. "How's the nose?"

"I'll live." He shrugged. "It'll give me an air of danger, don't you think?"

She chuckled. "Probably intimidate your students."

"What students?" He cocked his head. "You think I'm a teacher?"

She backpedaled. "Well, you ask a lot of questions. It seemed as good a guess as any."

"Were you guessing what I do?"

"No." She felt the blush creep up her cheeks and was

grateful for the twilight. "It just seemed like the obvious choice is all."

"I wouldn't have pegged you for choosing the obvious." He passed her one of the glasses. She took a sip and let her gaze slide to the shore of the little cove.

"What do you do then?"

"Direct. I like that." He took a drink of the water and rolled the wine glass between his hands. "I am a teacher."

She punched him in the arm. "University?"

"Younger."

"College?"

"Younger."

"High school? Junior high?"

"I teach kindergarten."

Dawn laughed out loud. "Kindergarten?" She tried to picture the serious, studious guy before her surrounded by a bunch of screaming kids and all she came up with was Schwarzenegger in that silly movie where he tells the kids *It's not a tumor*.

Erik shrugged and grinned. "I don't have a job."

"You're not working right now?"

"No, I mean, every day I get up and go to my class, and those little souls stream in through the door, and... " He shrugged again. "There's nowhere else I'd want to be, nothing else I'd like to be doing. It never feels like a job."

"More of a calling." She gazed up at the sky and spotted the northern star.

He laughed and clinked his glass to hers. "I wouldn't go that far. It's just how I spend my days. So, you pegged me as some studious, dusty old University prof?"

"Not dusty," Dawn said with a grin. She brushed at some fluff on her arm. Below them, Megan and Jenny emerged from the wheelhouse and made their way to the bow. They sat and

Jenny placed her phone on the deck between them. Had Timothy asked them to turn the location on their phones off?

And then she paused and rewound the conversation. Something about the way *studious* came off Erik's lips made her nervous. Hoping her question wouldn't reveal her suspicions, she said, "You have an unusual accent. Northern European mainly but do I detect some Irish there as well?"

"Guilty," he said. "I grew up in Sweden but my mother was Irish. I teach in Boston."

"What are you doing here? It's not a school holiday, is it?"

"Sabbatical," he said.

Her spidey senses were tingling. It was none of her business but she pressed on. "Kindergarten research?"

Erik laughed, a full, genuine sound that came up from his belly and almost put her at ease. "No, personal reasons. Flexibility is one of the reasons I teach."

From a distance came the high-pitched whine of an outboard engine open to full power. The mouth of the cove into the open channel faced east and was almost under full darkness. Small patches of flat water reflected weak light, creating a pattern on the water where the current tore at the patches. The engine kicked down, became more of a throb, and crossed the first point of the cove. She checked her anxiety. *Fishermen.* Only someone out at night, maybe bowfishing. Then, the small craft turned and entered the cove.

"Someone's out late," Erik said.

"Fishermen, likely," she said, trying to keep her rising anxiety out of her voice. The boat continued to approach them. "Or some pleasure boaters responding to the damn posts." She spied Jenny's form on the bow with distaste, then stretched toward the starboard and swung herself over the roof and down into the wheelhouse through the open door.

"Whoa," she heard Erik say behind her.

"We have company," she said. But her words echoed in the

empty wheelhouse. Timothy wasn't there. Cursing under her breath, she watched the boat come closer to the Papa Joe. She flicked on the spotlight and trained it on the small boat.

Three men. Not fishermen. They didn't look like pleasure boaters or even kids out for a joy ride. The two in front looked like thugs.

CHAPTER TWENTY-SIX

THE GUY IN THE BACK SEAT OF THE SMALL BOAT KEPT HIS head down, his neck twisted hard to the right to keep the light out of his eyes. The guy in the mate's chair and the guy driving held their hands up to their foreheads, shielding their eyes against the bright spotlight.

The captain kicked the outboard down to idle and they floated several meters off the starboard side.

"State your business," Dawn called out, infusing her voice with as much authority as she could.

"You're the Papa Joe?"

"State your business," Dawn repeated, her eyes darting quickly to each figure in the boat.

Hurried footsteps along the starboard side were followed by Timothy's head poking in the door. "Dawn, it's our late student."

She turned to him, her hands growing clammy. "What?"

"He texted me a few hours ago. They were planning to meet us at the other location before you insisted on moving."

"And you didn't tell me this because ... ?"

"You've been so weird about our location, I figured you'd say no."

"Damn right I would have said no." She clenched her jaw and the muscles in her neck tightened. "Cripes, Timothy—"

"You're over-reacting," he said. "Having that student step onboard now brings us several hundred more dollars."

"Papa Joe, permission to board," yelled out the captain, edging the boat toward their starboard side.

Dawn struggled to control her breathing. Erik yelled down from above. "Want me to grab the line?" On the bow, Megan watched while Jenny snapped photos with her phone.

Shaking her head, Dawn shoved down the ball of fear rising from her belly and pointed the spotlight on the water, providing a path for them to advance.

"You're an asshole," she hissed. "And this isn't over."

Timothy grunted. "With you it never is." He returned aft.

Without the light in his eyes, the missing student raised his head. His face was in shadow, but his eyes darted wildly side to side and up to Dawn in the wheelhouse. His mouth hung open, slack. He looked drunk. Or high. The last thing she needed was to add somebody out of control to the mix she already had onboard.

"Throw me a line," Timothy said.

"No need," said the guy sitting in the mate's chair. "We'll just come up alongside."

"Let me see your hands," Dawn said. The men in front shrugged and raised their hands.

"Dawn." Timothy hissed at her and shook his head. "They're just dropping off the student."

"Quiet," she said, the blood rushing loudly into her ears. "The guy in back... yes, you, show me your hands."

As they edged along the starboard hull, the light from the galley window fell onto the student's face. Dawn gasped. His lower lip was busted open. A yellowish bruise near his left temple and his brow told her his lid would swell and close before long.

He shook his head and raised his shoulders. His arms were tight behind his back. He was bound. Dawn's legs went weak and time slowed.

"Timothy," she yelled, "push them off."

CHAPTER TWENTY-SEVEN

"Too late, sunshine," said the driver, standing and leveling a gun toward Erik and Timothy at the stern. "Now you can toss us a line, Timothy."

Laughing, he turned back to Dawn. "Permission to come aboard, Captain."

The man in the mate's chair leaped aboard while the Captain waved his gun at Erik and Timothy. "Back up, give Jose some room," he said. Once Jose had the line cleated off, the man with the gun boarded.

His attention focused on his feet for a few seconds, Dawn stepped toward the forward cabin. "Go get Captain Sunshine before she does anything stupid," he barked. Moments later, Jose burst into the wheelhouse and grabbed her roughly, digging his fingers into her upper arm. She itched to punch him but having a gun aimed at her passengers was a game changer.

"I've got your buddies here ready to walk the plank," the man with the gun said. "Don't try anything heroic, Captain."

Dawn allowed herself to be guided back to the stern. She noticed the light in the galley had been shut off. Shooting Timothy a look that would kill, she took a place beside him.

Tilting his head toward the bow, the man said, "Get those two up on the bow and bring them back here."

Jose left to get the two women up front. For now, they didn't seem to know about the Howes. Dawn slanted a look toward the galley and Erik caught her glance. His eyes met hers. She was hoping against hope that Mr. Howe might keep a cool head and get them out of this. For now, Howe had the element of surprise working to his advantage.

"You're hurting me," Jenny said, as she was pushed onto the stern. She stumbled into Timothy, who caught her elbow and righted her.

"Only one of them, Miguel" Jose said. "The other can't be far."

"Find her," Miguel said. "Be quick about it." Turning his dark brown eyes on Timothy, he indicated the line coiled on the stern. "Get to work tying these folks up." He pointed the gun at Dawn. "Start with her."

Timothy stepped behind her and she held her hands together behind her back. Ice coursed through her veins and her mind raced looking for a way to overtake the men. As Timothy started to loop the rope around them, she measured the distance between herself and Miguel. Six feet. Could she rush him before he had a chance to shoot her? She'd need a way to distract him.

"I'll be checking your work later," Miguel said to Timothy. "Make a proper knot."

The acrid smell of Timothy's fear filled her nostrils, his hands clammy against her skin. Dawn clenched her wrists, tensing her muscles are much as possible, while Timothy tightened the rope against her skin. Tight, but not digging in. She hoped to hell he would realize what she was doing. She felt his finger tip against her back. He was drawing something. Or writing something. A letter. She tried to following the pressure of his finger against her skin.

Miguel, keeping his back to the cabin, edged over toward them. "Hurry up." He jutted his chin toward Erik and kicked at his foot. "Sit down. You, too," he said to Jenny. "Back to back." Erik and Jenny dropped to the deck, Jenny's face white as snow.

Timothy tried one final time to leave her a message, his finger tip trailing over her back. Miguel waved the gun at him. "I said hurry the hell up. Are you hard of hearing?"

"Go," Dawn said under her breath.

"These two, they can link their arms and then you tie them around the chest." Erik reached back and linked his elbows through Jenny's arms, then Timothy knelt and wound the rope around their torsos.

"Good enough." Miguel reached forward and tilted Jenny's chin up toward him. "Hmm, a pretty one." He wiggled his brows in an exaggerated way and blew her a kiss. Jenny turned away, her eyes wide with fear.

Miguel laughed, a harsh sound in the stillness of the little cove and stepped to the side. "Jose, what the hell? Did the girl take you out?"

Jose's voice came from above. Dawn glanced up at the roof. "She's gone."

"What the hell do you mean, gone?"

He shrugged. "I can't find her. She's not here."

"You looked everywhere?"

Jose nodded.

Out of the corner of her eye, Dawn caught a small movement of Jenny's head. She turned to her. *Water*, Jenny mouthed. Megan had gone overboard?

Miguel erupted. "Well the girl didn't vanish into thin air."

"She's not here." Jose's voice had an edge to it.

"Fine, get down here and tie up the last one." Miguel waved his gun at Timothy. "Sit down."

Timothy's eyes narrowed. "Piss off," he said.

Miguel backhanded him behind the ear.

"What the—" Timothy jumped backward out of his reach. He was hopping mad, as mad as the day he'd found out about his engine, bouncing his weight from one foot to the other. "What the hell do you want? We have a few electronics and maybe a little bit of cash. You can have it. Take it all." He turned to the boat tied up alongside and yelled down at the missing student. "What the hell were you thinking? Hiring these morons to bring you out here? Look at the trouble you caused."

Miguel rolled back on his heels and barked out a laugh. "He didn't hire us." Dawn's belly clenched as she caught his faint Cuban accent. "We intercepted him earlier this morning so we could find you. He's had a lovely day entertaining us while we waited for you to send your location."

His mouth twisted cruelly as he sneered at Timothy. "You played right into our hands, cowboy."

CHAPTER TWENTY-EIGHT

Dawn watched Timothy's face cave in as he realized he was responsible for the danger he'd put them all in. If she hadn't wanted to kill him in this moment, she might have felt sorry for him. He slanted her a look but she refused to meet his eye. She struggled to breathe. These were the men Duncan had warned her about. On her boat. With weapons.

Here she sat in the middle of freaking nowhere, with nobody to help them, and six other souls on board her vessel that she was responsible for. She swallowed hard, tamping down the fear crawling up her throat. With any luck, they'd shoot her and just carry on. The others didn't deserve to be in the middle of this.

Her mind raced ahead of itself. Timothy was still standing. If he was able to knock Miguel off balance, even for a few seconds, she could body check Jose. She couldn't let her anger with Timothy get in the way. If she'd been more forthcoming with him, they may not be in this mess.

Right now Timothy presented an opportunity and perhaps their only chance. She tried to catch his eye, but he kept his head down. Silently she cursed him, her anger flaring again.

"Tie him up," Miguel said. He leaned back against the ladder, his arm hanging down loosely, the gun resting against his thigh. His heavy-lidded eyes roved over the group.

Jose leaned down in front of Timothy to pick up the rope. Quick as a flash, Timothy stepped forward, pushed the back of Jose's neck down, and brought his knee up into his face. Jose stumbled backward. It was all Dawn needed. She rolled onto her feet and rushed forward, hurling her right shoulder toward Miguel's chest. Her feet left the deck, for a moment she was weightless, then her body smashed into Miguel's side.

He grunted as the force of her body slamming into him pushed his breath out but she hadn't been fast enough. His arm was already raised above her and he brought the butt of the gun down toward her face. At the last second, she jerked her head to the side and it cracked against her temple. Bile rushed to her mouth as pain shivered through her. She'd missed her mark. Regret washed through her. Stunned, she slumped to the deck and he placed his boot on her neck.

"Don't mess with me, Sunshine." His eyes glinted cold as steel as he stared down at her, his nostrils flaring. "I have a job to do but I can always tell the boss you went overboard and I wasn't able to bring you in."

"Miguel!" yelled Jose. Timothy straddled Jose, his arm drawn back, fist clenched, ready to throw a punch.

Miguel leaned into Timothy's sightline, the gun pointed at his face. "I suggest you get up now. Very slowly."

Lips curled back, exposing his teeth, Timothy growled. They locked eyes while Timothy pushed himself up to his feet.

"Back away, go on, over near the tall guy. Sit down." Miguel's voice, laced with menace, left no room for argument.

Timothy edged away until he was next to Erik then folded himself cross-legged onto the deck. Erik's eyes were wide, Jenny's face ashen, her lip trembling. "Jose, get this asshole tied up. Now."

Brushing himself off, Jose got up, grabbed the line and stalked over to Timothy. He kicked him in the ribs, and Timothy lurched and fell over sideways. Jose landed another kick at his kidneys, ordered him up, wound the line around his chest several times with his arms tight against his sides, and tied the rope off at the back.

Miguel's boot weighing on her windpipe, Dawn struggled to breath. She caught Timothy's eye briefly but he was defeated. At least he'd tried. She'd give him that. "Can't breathe," she choked out, twisting her head to look up at Miguel.

His cruel laugh jarred her. "Air. It's free, right? We don't give it a second thought until it's not available." He quirked his brow. "Are you able to behave yourself if I remove my foot?"

A nasty retort rushed to Dawn's lips but she held it back, feeling the cloak of unconsciousness about to settle over her. She needed to stay calm. And she needed oxygen. Now. She nodded.

"Use your words," he said, grinning down at her. A gold cap on his right incisor glinted as his grin spread wider.

"Yes," she hissed. He lifted his foot, releasing the pressure on her neck, then ran the toe of his boot over the crest of her right breast while keeping his eyes on hers. Every muscle in her body tightened but she refused to flinch, determined not to give him the satisfaction of shaking her.

"Jose, tie this wench to something so she doesn't move around again." He pointed to one of the stern cleats. "That should work."

He turned his attention back to Dawn. "Get over there. Now." He kicked her in the butt as she scrambled away from him on her knees, sending her sprawling across the deck.

Jose laughed. "Good one."

In the corner of the stern, Jose looped another line around her wrists and tied her taut to the cleat. Her arms and shoulders were pulled backward, her back slightly arched, her butt barely on the deck. She braced her feet trying to relieve some of the strain.

"What about him?" Jose said, motioning to the late student on the speedboat. His head lolled to the side, he was barely conscious. He hadn't made a peep. "Should I bring him up?"

Miguel shrugged. "Nah, there's enough people to deal with up here. Leave him there for the night."

Jose stepped over to Miguel and dropped his voice. "What's your plan here? I thought we were just supposed to bring her in?"

"We're here now," Miguel said, "might as well make it worth our while, have a little fun. Besides, as our friend here pointed out," he slanted a look at Timothy, "there's a few valuables on board we may be interested in. We can consider that as bonus pay."

"Boss won't be happy about this," Jose said.

Miguel stepped closer to him. He towered over him by a head. "Right now I'm your boss," he said. He stared at Jose until the other man looked away.

"Besides," Miguel continued, "I think we should have a little fun." His eyes dipped toward Jenny. Jose followed his gaze and leered at Jenny.

"There *were* two, one for each of us," Miguel continued, "but you seem to have lost the other one." He closed the distance between himself and Jenny, running a strand of her hair through his fingers. "I guess we'll have to share this one."

Dawn's stomach clenched. Not on her watch.

Jenny pulled her head to the side. "Leave me alone," she said sharply.

Miguel clenched his hand into her hair, grabbed a fistful and yanked her head backward so she was looking up at him. "Pretty and feisty," he said. "Just how I like them."

Jenny's lower lip trembled, but her eyes snapped with electricity. "Get your hands off me."

"Maybe I'll have the captain," Jose said. He moved toward Dawn.

"Yes," Dawn hissed. She'd have more of a chance with them than Jenny would. "You're here for me, so leave the others out of it."

"Shut up." Miguel shook his head. "No." He held up his hand to Jose, who stopped mid-step. "We don't touch the Captain. She's our payday. She's coming with us later."

"Listen," Dawn said.

Miguel glared at her. "Keep it up, sunshine and things can go much worse for everybody. I promise."

Dawn's blood boiled but she bit back her words.

Miguel puckered his lips and blew a kiss down to Jenny before releasing her roughly.

He waved a hand toward the bow. "Sweep the boat again, the other one can't be far away."

CHAPTER TWENTY-NINE

Dawn gaze swept the shore, eyes straining for any flicker of movement. If Megan had escaped overboard, she must have gone somewhere. She hoped she was safe. Her impression of her was that she was level-headed, but she had no idea how strong a swimmer she might be.

Peering into the darkness, she saw the branch of a small shrub move at the far end of a rocky beach. Her hopes up, she leaned forward, but no. It was only a sandpiper hopping toward the shore.

Miguel had returned to his favored spot, lounging against the ladder, his gun now tucked away. She had a view of Erik and Jenny in profile, they both glanced her way repeatedly. Helpless, she had no answers for them.

Meanwhile, Timothy kept his head down and avoided her gaze. Whatever embarrassment or shame he was feeling, he was going to have to get over it, because if they were going to get out of this, she needed him.

Again, Jose's voice came from the top deck. "Nothing. She's not here." He climbed down the ladder and Miguel shifted to the side to let him pass. "However, I couldn't get into this cabin." He patted the aft cabin with his palm and moved to the door where he tried the knob. Locked.

"What? You didn't check it earlier?" Miguel grumbled something colorful in Spanish under his breath. "Why am I always saddled with the stupid ones?"

"I'm not stupid," Jose said.

"Then why didn't you check?"

He shrugged. Miguel shook his head again and huffed out a breath. His gaze swung to Dawn. "Why is this cabin locked? What's in there?"

"It's the galley," Dawn said. "We lock it up at night."

"With this many people on board? You must take me for an idiot. Where are the keys?"

Dawn bit her lip to buy some time, then raised her voice. "The key to the galley is on the keyring in the small box next to the wheel. In the wheelhouse." Timothy peered up at her from beneath heavy brows. She hoped Mr. Howe would hear her and be ready when they entered. If he could take one of them out, they might have a chance. Timothy's chin tilted upward and his eyes shot to the door.

Jose hurried up along the side to the wheelhouse and returned with the key. He inserted it into the lock.

"Hang on," Miguel whispered. "I'll go in first." He leveled the gun ahead of him, then nodded to Jose to unlock and open the door.

Jose swung the door back and Miguel charged in with the gun. Dawn held her breath.

Moments later, the light flicked on and Miguel's loud laughter rang through the air.

"Winston, there's a strange man in our cabin."

The glimmer of hope Dawn had nurtured dimmed. Mr. Howe wasn't about to step into the hero's role.

Miguel returned to the aft deck, laughing so hard tears

streamed down his face. "They were dead to the world," he said. "Fudging the truth a little there, Captain? Galley closed up for the night?"

She narrowed her eyes and said, "Don't hurt them."

"Jose, get them out of bed and bring them out here with the rest of this bunch of losers."

"Now see here, young man—" Winston's voice was drowned out by Jose's as he ordered them out of bed and out onto the deck. Mrs. Howe argued she needed her robe before she could get up. Jose barked more orders and Mr. Howe stumbled out the door as Jose pushed him, with Mrs. Howe following closely on his heels.

They both wore fluorescent green silicon ear plugs. Mrs. Howe had an eye mask pushed up onto her head. One hung loosely below Mr. Howe's chin. No wonder they'd slept through it. They took in their boat mates bound on the deck as if they'd been invited late to a murder mystery dinner then both their eyes widened as their gazes fixed on Miguel and the gun in his hand.

"Sit down on the deck," he said. "Back to back. Jose, more rope."

Jose dug under the stern and found another line. A couple of minutes later, he had them bound. Mrs. Howe started to sob. When Dawn shushed her, the woman's look almost broke her heart. She clearly was barely awake.

Miguel surveyed the lot of them and tucked the gun into the waistband at the back of his pants. "I need a drink." Jose followed him into the galley. Cabinet doors opened and thudded closed, followed by the clinking of bottles, the fridge being opened, glasses and utensils.

"She's deeply sedated," Mr. Howe said, cranking his neck to see Dawn. "She may look awake, but she's barely here." It took Dawn a second to realize he was talking about his wife.

"Sleeping pill," he added, by way of explanation. "What the bloody hell is going on out here?"

"Quiet," Timothy said. Miguel's shadow fell over them as he stepped back into the doorway.

"What do you have for grub? Something quick 'n easy." His eyes slid to Jenny. "Don't worry sweetheart, I'll still have an appetite for your brand of quick 'n easy." Jenny's chest heaved and she squeezed her eyes shut. Dawn dug her nails so hard into her palms she almost broke the skin.

"You," Miguel pointed at Timothy, while the sound of things being piled on the cupboard behind him floated into the air. "What is there to eat?"

"Some snacks in the top cupboard, over the bunk," Timothy said. "Chips, crackers. Cheese in the fridge." He spat the words out. "Make yourself at home."

Miguel laughed. "Thanks, we will." He turned and leaned against the door jamb watching Jose find the food. When he turned back, he held a large bag of chips in his hand. He popped one in his mouth, then stepped over to Dawn, holding another one out to her. "Hungry?"

She shook her head.

"I think you are." He butted the chip up against her lips. "Eat it." She turned her head away. "Eat the damn chip," he said, his breath hot against her forehead. Reluctantly, she parted her lips and he shoved it in her mouth.

"Say what you will about me, but Mama taught me to share." His eyes slid over toward Jenny again. "But don't worry darling, I'm not so polite that I plan to share you. You I plan to have all to myself."

Goosebumps ran down Jenny's arm as she trembled. Erik leaned slightly into her, pressing his back to hers. For comfort, Dawn supposed, to remind her he was there, that she wasn't alone. Even though she surely knew he couldn't help her.

But when Miguel untied Jenny, he'd have to untie Erik at the same time. Erik caught Dawn's eye and dropped a lid in a half-wink. She was certain he was thinking the same thing.

These guys were assholes, but they clearly hadn't thought much of this through.

Which meant an opportunity would present itself, and she planned to be ready for it.

CHAPTER THIRTY

"Open up." Miguel aimed a chip at Timothy's mouth. It bounced off Timothy's cheek and onto the deck. Miguel shook his head. "Wasteful." He shouted out to Jose. "These ungrateful sods are wasteful."

Returning his attention to Timothy, he said, "You're going to be hungry later and wish you'd eaten these chips."

"Idiot." Timothy spoke softly but Dawn heard him. Miguel did too. What the hell was Timothy thinking?

"Idiot? Let's see about that." He kicked at Timothy's hip. "Up on your knees," he said. Timothy struggled to rock up onto his knees, his torso bound tightly with rope. Miguel stood over him, his thick thighs inches from Timothy's chin. "Tilt your head back."

Dawn watched in horror, dreading a scene from Deliverance. Behind Timothy, the Howes' mouths dropped in unison. Jenny turned her head away and Erik caught Dawn's eye.

"Open your mouth."

"Screw you," Timothy said.

Miguel whacked him upside the head. His body swayed to the left before he righted himself.

"Tilt your head back," Miguel said, enunciating each word carefully, "and then, open your mouth."

"Never."

Crack. Timothy's head snapped to the side as Miguel's fist made solid contact with his upper cheekbone.

"Leave him alone," Dawn said. "What the hell, he can't even fight back."

"Captain, I'd advise you to shut the hell up." Miguel slanted her a quick look before turning his focus back on Timothy. Timothy's skin had split open and a trickle of blood trailed down the side of his face. Miguel grabbed a fistful of his hair, as he had with Jenny, and pulled his head cruelly back on his neck until Timothy's jaw dropped and his mouth open.

Dawn held her breath.

"Now bark like a seal."

Wait, what?

Miguel jerked Timothy's head. "Bark!"

"Arrr, arr." Timothy barked, his eyes closed. Color crept up his cheeks.

Dawn bit back her words worried anything she might say now would only inflame Miguel.

Miguel dropped a chip into Timothy's mouth and roared with laughter. "Good boy," he said. "Bark again."

Timothy's Adam's apple bobbed in his stretched neck as he tried to swallow. Miguel clenched his fist in his hair and tugged backwards. "Bark."

"Arr, arr."

Miguel dropped another chip, then another, and then a handful, until Timothy's mouth was full. The chips slid down his face, clung to his shirt, and scattered onto the dock. "So wasteful. Jose, come and see this." He released his grip on Timothy's hair and Timothy spat a mouthful of chips out.

"I don't think so," Miguel said. "Waste not, want not." He

grabbed his hair again and slammed his body forward, his forehead hitting the deck with a loud crack. Timothy grunted.

"Not a grunt, how about an oink?"

Timothy squeezed his eyes tighter.

"Open your eyes, little piggy. How will you see the chips? I want nothing wasted." Holding his hand against the back of Timothy's head, he guided him to a pile of chips. "Eat."

Dawn's eyes moistened. She didn't care much for Timothy but Miguel was purposefully humiliating him. For no good reason other than it entertained him. Was he high?

With his lips and tongue, Timothy picked at the chips, chewed and swallowed. One by one they started to disappear from the deck.

"Now oink, little piggy."

Jose leaned against the doorway, slugging down a cold beer. "That's funny shit," he said to Miguel. "I didn't realize you had a sense of humor."

"Of course I have a sense of humor," Miguel said. "Oink," he repeated to Timothy who shook his head. Miguel grabbed his hair again and shook Timothy's head violently in an up down motion. "When I tell you to do something, you say yes. Never no. Never, ever no. Understand?"

Timothy went still. Miguel cracked his head into the deck again. "Oink."

All was silent.

Miguel banged his head down again. "Oink."

A grunt escaped Timothy's lips and blood spattered across the deck.

Once more, Miguel slammed his head down into the deck.

Dawn growled.

Everyone froze. In the stillness of the night, Timothy's voice broke as he said, "Oink."

"Quite the farmyard. Pigs and seals, living together in harmony." He upended the bag under Timothy's face. "When I get back, little piggy, I want all of this cleaned up. Little oinker. What did you find for us to eat, Jose?"

"Um, some crackers and cheese. Pickles, olives, that kind of thing. Want some?"

"Hell yeah, I have an appetite now," Miguel said. He stepped through the door of the galley then glanced back over his shoulder and sneered. "Animals."

Dawn let out the breath she'd been holding as he went through the door, but he pivoted and came back out. She glanced over at Timothy. She wasn't sure he could take much more

"So, if the other woman isn't on the boat, what happened to her?" He stood in front of Dawn, his stance wide. "Is there a cubby on the boat? Somewhere she could be hiding?"

"No. Nowhere big enough for a person."

"I'll look, you know. And if I find one, and if I find her—"

"She went overboard." Jenny tilted her chin and looked him right in the eye.

"What's that, Princess? I didn't realize you could form full sentences. How delightful." He turned in her direction. "Where did she go?"

"I... I don't know. I think she's dead. She can't swim." Jenny's face crumpled, and a tear slid down her cheek.

"Someone who can't swim went overboard? I've heard it all now."

"She was terrified," Jenny said. "She can't swim. She almost drowned earlier today. Ask them."

"It's true," Erik said. "I had to go in after her."

"Finally, a hero in this bunch of morons. So where's her body? She should have floated to the top by now."

"We haven't exactly been paying attention to that," Erik said.

Miguel stepped over to Jenny, his thigh pressing against her shoulder. She turned her head away. "Honey." His fingers gripped her chin and tilted her face up toward him. "If you're lying to me, things will go very badly for you later."

"It's the truth," she sputtered. "He had to go in and save her. She almost drown and now... " She sobbed loudly. "Now my friend is dead."

Leaning over, Miguel put his face nose-to-nose with Jenny. "Cheer up, honey," he said, one finger trailing down over the crest of her breast. "I'm going to give you something to live for as soon as I have a snack." He cupped his crotch and laughed at his own joke.

Without another word, he returned to the galley.

Tears streamed down Jenny's face as she shook from head to toe.

Dawn strained against the ropes that held her tight to the cleat. These people were her responsibility and she was failing them.

CHAPTER THIRTY-ONE

THE HORIZON HAD COMPLETELY DARKENED, THE SKY ABOVE an inky palette for the stars strewn upon it. Jenny sobbed pitifully in the night and Dawn waited for the men inside the galley to resume their conversation.

Jose said something that made Miguel laugh and Dawn hissed in Jenny's direction. "Megan can't swim?" She found that hard to believe given how comfortable and capable she'd seemed on the boat.

Jenny looked up, sniffed and shook her head.

"No she can't swim or no, she can swim?" Dawn glanced meaningful toward the galley door. She didn't know how long they had. Although it had been Timothy who'd revealed their location, Dawn had zero doubts in her mind that she was responsible for these mean bastards being on her boat. They'd been sent to collect her. She only wished they'd stuck to their plan, collected her and left everyone else alone.

"She can swim," Jenny whispered. "She went overboard."

"Where is she?" Dawn asked.

Jenny shrugged and looked out over the water. Her face was streaked with tears. "He's, he's… "

"We're not going to let him hurt you," Erik said.

Jenny's head swung back to Dawn.

"What he said," Dawn said. "We won't let it happen." She knew as the words left her mouth, that she had no way to back them up, but she had to say something. She only hoped it wasn't an outright lie and she'd somehow find a way to protect Jenny.

Despite the obvious, that they had no way to help her while they were tied up, Jenny's chest stopped heaving and her sobs subsided. "She used to be a lifeguard."

Even better. Wherever Megan was, she was probably safe so at least one of them was off the boat. Maybe she'd be able to go for help. Dawn looked toward the shore again. She knew there were no residences on this little island. It was big enough but it formed part of a nature reserve. And it was highly unlikely that a ranger would come by to check on things at this time of night.

Perhaps Megan would find someone illegally camping or another boat anchored somewhere along the shoreline. Surely she was taking some action to get them help. Dawn wondered if she'd been able to go overboard with a phone, but dismissed the thought, given how quickly things had happened. She remembered her sitting on the bow with Jenny, and doubted she'd be able to keep a phone dry if she'd gone over.

Timothy lifted his head. He'd been quiet. His humiliation had been complete, a horror to watch. Nobody should be treated that way. "One of us has to get loose," he said.

"How?" she whispered.

Without hesitation, Timothy tipped his head toward Jenny. "He's coming back for her. Maybe she can take him out."

Jenny's mouth dropped. "I can't. I'm not strong enough."

"You can't put her in that position," Erik said. Behind him, Mr. Howe watched the conversation like a tennis tournament, Mrs. Howe slumped against his back, her sleeping pills having kicked in again.

"Wait," Dawn said. "Timothy's right. She doesn't have to take him out, but we might have a chance when he comes to untie her." She looked at Erik. "He's going to have to untie you, too."

"What's going on out here?" Jose appeared in the doorway. "Any more talk, and I'll put one of you overboard." He stepped back inside while Miguel laughed behind him.

Glass clinked against glass as they helped themselves to more of their booze. Given how Miguel had already treated Timothy, Dawn hoped he wasn't a mean drunk.

"I have an idea," Mr. Howe whispered. All heads turned in his direction. As Dawn watched, he lifted his shoulders and raised his hands in the air. "I think I can slide out of this rope."

"Really?" Jenny leaned forward and scrutinized the rope.

"It's really loose. Once he unties you, if Erik can distract him, I can get loose."

"And then what?" Timothy asked.

Mr. Howe's bushy brows met over the bridge of his nose. "I'm quite strong," he said. "I might look soft, but I train three times a week, and I play polo. I'm very agile."

The others stared at him. Dawn said, "Good. It sounds like a decent plan."

Jenny's shoulders dropped. She didn't quite smile, but hope crept into her face. Erik twisted his head and spoke to Jenny. "We won't let anything happen to you." Turning back to Howe, he said, "When they untie Jenny, I'll be loose for a few minutes. I'll do what I can to take them off guard, and Mr. Howe, you use that time to get loose."

"And then what?" Timothy asked again.

"Then we'll be one-on-one," Mr. Howe said.

"They still have a gun," Timothy said, as if any of them could forget.

"I'm not going to sit here and do nothing," Mr. Howe said, an edge to his voice.

"It's something," Dawn said. "We have to take whatever opportunity we get."

Inside a burst of laughter was followed by silence. Dawn sat stock still, her ears straining to see if one of them would come back outside. When the men's conversation resumed, she nodded and looked at each of her fellow passengers. "Be ready."

Timothy was right. It wasn't much of a plan but it was all they had and action would give them hope.

CHAPTER THIRTY-TWO

MEGAN WRAPPED HER FINGERS AROUND THE PLATFORM AT the stern of the boat and lay perfectly still in the calm sea. Despite the initial warmth of the water, she was cold and shivering, her fingers puckered like prunes. The night air was warm and she considered lifting herself onto the platform for a while.

Above her, all was mostly quiet. The two strangers were inside the galley. She wished there was a way to communicate with Dawn, but she couldn't risk it. Pushing off from the platform, she moved slowly, heart pounding in her throat, careful not to make a ripple, along the hull of the Papa Joe until she reached the speedboat, then she made her way to the far side until she was directly below the man they'd left in the boat.

She looked up at him. His head rested against the gunwale. Dried blood caked his blonde hair. The eye she could see was closed, puffy, the skin around it swollen, yellow and purple. His breathing was ragged, shallow, like a cheese grater in the night. She hissed up at him but he didn't move.

She didn't know how much time she had, they could come back outside at any moment. She hissed again, a little louder, but again no response. Pushing herself along the side of the boat to the bow, she looked for a way to get onboard where she couldn't be seen and wouldn't make noise. The bow was too high off the water. She returned to the back. Her best bet would be to go in over the stern, on the far side of the large outboard.

Hanging off the stern, she listened. Someone on the back deck was talking in whispers. Inside the two men were laughing, their crude voices carrying out over the water.

She calculated her options carefully. If she slipped, she'd make big splash and then it would be over. She'd heard Miguel say the other man could have her. That wasn't going to happen.

Wrapping her hands around the gunwale above, she pushed herself up until her she was balanced half in and half out of the water. Water dripped off her legs onto the calm surface, sounding like bullets in the oppressive silence. Under her weight, the boat shifted and rocked away from the Papa Joe. She froze for two heartbeats, then, before it could roll back, she reached her hands down to the deck and walked herself with her hands into the bottom of the boat.

The speedboat rolled back and squashed the bumper along the side. Megan pressed along the port side, stretching her body as flat as possible against the side. Still unconscious, the passenger didn't flinch.

Heavy footsteps from above and then a shadow fell over the boat. She held her breath, blood pounding in her ears.

"There's nothing," Jose said. "Just a wave or something." He turned his attention to the others on the back deck. "You guys better not be moving around. Don't try anything, you hear?"

He laughed, louder than was necessary, and returned to the galley. Seconds later, the men clinked glasses and returned to their conversation. They were starting to get drunk.

On her hands and knees, Megan scrambled over to the man and placed her hand lightly over his mouth while she lifted his chin. His face was a mess. She tapped his cheek, still no reaction. She pinched his inner thigh. His eyes flew open, disoriented, and he looked around. A beat later, panic flared in his eyes as he remembered where he was.

Megan put a finger to her lips. "I'm here to help," she whispered. "Nod if you understand." She wasn't sure if they'd drugged him. He seemed pretty out of it.

He nodded and she removed her hand from his mouth.

"Water." The man lifted his head, fixed Megan with his eyes. His lips were dry, cracked.

"Let me find something." She checked all the cupholders and came up empty. There was nothing in the compartments along the sides or at the stern. A small cubby at the front of the boat held only a bottle of rum and a few warm cans of beer. She popped the top on one of the beers and brought it back to him. "This is all I could find."

"Bill." He croaked out his name, wrapped his hand around the can, tilted his head and drank deeply, the suds trickling down his chin. He swallowed and coughed.

Megan slapped her hand over his mouth and shushed him. She grabbed the can and wedged herself against the compartment closest to the hull of the Papa Joe and held her breath.

"What's going on out here?" The tallest of the two men, the one his friend called Miguel, stepped out of the galley and cast an eye around the people assembled there. Dawn in the far corner, Timothy, Erik and Jenny tied together and close to them the Howes, also tied back to back. She held her breath.

"A tickle in my throat," Mr. Howe said.

Miguel arched a brow and turned away.

Megan exhaled. Staying low, she crawled back to Bill and passed him the beer. This time, he took long swallows instead of trying to chug it. "I'm Megan," she said. "My friends on the boat need our help."

"What did you have in mind?"

"I don't have a plan," she said, "at least, not right now. But

I'm not going to sit by while that asshole assaults Jenny." He passed her the empty can and she tucked it back in the forward cubby.

"Grab me another?"

"I need you sober," she said.

"I'm still thirsty. It's only beer."

"You're weak, dehydrated, probably haven't eaten all day. And there's only a few, so let's measure them out."

He cocked his head to the right. "See, you do have a plan."

"Did they drug you?"

"What?"

"Did they give you anything to make you pass out?"

"I don't know. I have a pretty bad headache."

"Right, dehydrated. I can't believe they left you unsheltered in the sun all day."

"That's the least of it," he said. He glanced up toward the boat. "On the way out here, I overheard some of what they're planning for the woman who owns this boat. We need to do something."

CHAPTER THIRTY-THREE

MIGUEL'S FIGURE FILLED THE GALLEY DOORWAY, THE LIGHT from behind casting a long shadow over the stern, leaving Timothy's face in darkness. He leaned casually against the door-frame, but his face was blotchy and pink, veins popped on his bulbous nose. His lips were garishly stained from red wine. A bottle swung from the fingers of his right hand. Letting his eyes run over each of them on the stern, he lifted the bottle, drained what was left of the wine, then tossed the bottle overboard. Timothy ducked as the bottle sailed mere inches above his head.

Dawn's jaw clenched. Timothy had tied her wrists loosely, with some kind of slipknot, and she'd been working the line for over an hour now. At certain angles, sharp pain forced her to rest, her wrist still sore from where Dylan had broken it. She kept at it. She definitely had more movement than before. She was still tied down tight to the cleat though, but it felt like that rope was looped through the one on her wrists. With more time, she would work herself free.

But she didn't have time.

Her shoulders were pulled back, blades practically touching, her hands tied to the cleat on the deck. Her whole upper body resembled a taut bow. The muscles in her back and shoulder strained with the constant stress of her position. She wasn't unfamiliar with pain. She'd made friends with it years ago in the ring. Pain motivated her, pushed her before her opponent could take her down. She tapped into that pain now as she leveled her gaze at Miguel. A fire burned in her belly as she strategized how she would take him out.

Her companions on the stern remained still and quiet. Timothy's face was still in shadow, but the profile of Erik was stoic while Jenny's head was down, hoping to avoid attention. Mrs. Howe slumbered against the back of her husband and Mr. Howe caught Dawn's eye. His lid lowered a fraction. He was ready.

The harbor entrance in the distance behind the Howes was a dark hole, so black it was inky, like a blank left to be filled in. The moon and the stars had been obscured behind a sea of dark, building clouds. The darkness pressed in on them.

"Hey Jose, pass me another bottle of wine." Miguel swung his attention toward the galley, then turned back toward her with a new bottle in his hand. He pushed himself away from the door, unsteady on his feet, and his free hand shot out to brace himself.

He was drunk. Having been flattened in more than one bar room brawl because of too much whisky, Dawn knew his inebriation would slow him down, make him sloppy, easier to throw off balance. He'd be quicker to anger. His hand-eye coordination would suffer. His thinking would be compromised. A little strategy and use of his own weight could give her an advantage despite his size.

Miguel stumbled to the bench to Dawn's left and sat heavily.

"Jose, Jose, come on out and play," he sang, laughing. He put the wine down on the bench, turned to Dawn and stroked her cheek with the back of his hand. "Hmmm. You're pretty too, but," he placed his finger to his lips, "boss wants you in tip top shape. So," he waved his finger in front of his face, "no, no, no. I can't have you." His eyes trailed down the front of her bowed torso. "Such a pity."

He cupped her chin in his hand and she braced herself. "What is so special about you, Dawn Devon? Hmmm? You just look like a slip of a girl to me. Sure you have a boat, and —" he waved sloppily toward the others "some friends. But the boss promised me a front row seat for later. What did he say, Jose?"

Jose leaned in the doorway and chuckled. "Seam by seam."

"Right." Miguel squeezed her chin until she flinched, then pushed her face away with his thumb. "Seam. By. Seam. I'm gonna enjoy watching that." He pushed himself to his feet then turned back and leaned into her face, his rancid breath filling her nostrils. "Hey, I may even get to help."

"I don't even know your boss," Dawn said, her mind racing for a way to delay him, to keep him talking.

"Oh, you know the boss," Jose said.

"Quiet." Miguel waved the bottle at Jose. "You always say too much."

Jose's brows shot up. Emboldened by the alcohol, he said, "You're the one who's doing the talking."

Miguel's forehead creased and a storm passed over his features. "Keep an eye on these losers," he said. "Time for me and Ginger to have some alone time." He stepped up onto the stern, but stumbled, his hand reaching for Erik's shoulder to brace himself. On one knee, he worked the rope tying Erik and Jenny together.

Dawn's eyes caught Erik's and she nodded slightly. Timothy shifted his legs, rolling his weight forward, ready to push himself up. Mr. Howe's face remained impassive but he inched his shoulders upwards in a barely perceptible movement. Dawn blinked.

Cursing, Miguel fumbled with the rope. Jenny had started to cry, her body shaking. "Stop moving," he yelled. He placed his face next to hers. "We're gonna have some fun, and I'm gonna want you to move. A lot. But right now I need you to stay still."

Jenny shook harder and her tears flowed more freely. Throwing his hands up in the air, Miguel yelled at Jose. "How the hell did you do this? Get over here and untie this mess."

Miguel slid off the deck and perched on the bench in front of Mr. Howe. Perfect. Erik leaned to the right so Jose could get to the ropes. Jenny fought to calm herself, her teeth clamped into her bottom lip. "There," Jose said, as the ropes fell free, "that wasn't so—"

Erik rolled in Jose's direction and body checked him with his shoulder. Jose lost his balance and Jenny turned and pushed him. He sprawled across the deck and Erik leaped onto his back.

"What the hell?" Miguel stepped forward and grabbed Erik's shirt to pull him off Jose. On the far deck, Mr. Howe struggled to get out of his ropes, failing. Mrs. Howe started and called her husband's name. Behind them, Dawn spotted another head poking up over the deck. The tardy student? Megan?

"Timothy, come on." Dawn struggled against the rope binding her to the cleat, the line digging deeply into her wrist. She ignored the pain.

Timothy was already rolling onto his knees. He lurched forward and tried to head butt Miguel, his forehead cracking against the side of his temple. Miguel stood back, surprise rippled across his face. For a moment he wavered like a large tree in the wind, then stumbled forward as Mrs. Howe kicked him solidly at the back of his knees.

He landed hard on the deck but rolled onto his side and barked out a laugh as he reach to his back and waved the gun at Timothy's face.

"Sit the hell back down," he said, through gritted teeth.

Then he plunged the butt of the pistol into Erik's back. Erik froze in place.

"And you, hero boy, get off Jose." Erik rolled to the side, and Jose turned over, his nose bloody. His hand shot up and he grabbed Erik by the throat, squeezing. Erik slammed his arm down, breaking Jose's hold, but not before Jose's nails broke his skin and left blood trailing down his neck.

"Hero boy, sit the hell down," Miguel said. He stepped into Erik's line of vision and waved the gun in his face.

Dawn's heart banged against her chest. He was too drunk, too volatile. Anything could happen. She worked furiously at the rope behind her. "Hey Miguel," she yelled, hoping to throw him off guard.

He speared her with a look. "Shut up, Sunshine. Unless you want me to put your lights out." Turning back to Erik, he said, "Sit the hell down."

Erik sat and Jose wound rope around his chest, binding his arms to his torso.

Miguel swung toward Mrs. Howe. "And you," he said, stepping ominously close to her. The woman cringed against her husband. "Good kick. I didn't know you had it in you." He patted her hair, an oddly intimate gesture and cocked his head. "You look a little like my dead granny."

"I'm sure she's proud of you," Mrs. Howe said, her lips thin.

"Don't push it, grandma," Miguel said, raising his arm. Mrs. Howe blanched. Miguel spat and pivoted away from her.

Jenny had shuffled herself to the very back of the stern. Dawn saw her glance at the water as Miguel stepped toward her. He reached out his hand, like he was asking her for a dance at a fine ball, and said, "My lady."

She shook her head. He slapped an open palm across her face. Hard. The sound reverberated through the night as they all held their breath. Jenny cried out and Miguel dragged her across the deck. Jenny clasped her hands to the stern, screaming, until he yanked her legs and she lost her grip. Her forehead hit the deck with a crack, and he pulled her, limp and sobbing, to a standing position.

Pushing her before him, they passed before Dawn and made their way down the port side. She tried to catch Jenny's eye but Jenny's eyes were fixed to the deck at her feet and full of tears.

As they stumbled away, Miguel yelled back over his shoulder. "Jose, you're in charge back here."

CHAPTER THIRTY-FOUR

JOSE LOUNGED AGAINST THE LADDER, HIS BACK TO THE speedboat. Megan motioned to Bill to keep an eye on him and then crawled, as low as she possibly could, across to the cubby hole. She backed inside where she had a view of Jose.

"Why didn't you go?" Bill whispered.

Megan grimaced. Adrenalin pumped through her. She'd been ready to leap onto the boat. "I couldn't get past the Howes. He was supposed to get up but couldn't get loose."

"I have eyes, I saw what happened," Bill hissed. "But we should have done something."

"We didn't have a chance." Her eyes shifted to Jose's back. "What's the point in them having us all captive?" Bill was starting to piss her off. He wasn't accomplishing anything more than she was, but she needed him to keep a level head for the next part. He continued to be groggy and nod off. She was almost certain they'd given him something.

"I'm going back in the water. Keep an eye on Jose."

"It'll make too much noise," he said. "The weight will rock the boats."

"We have to risk it." If they came back on the speedboat for any reason, they'd find her and their chance would be lost.

"Jose," Miguel yelled. She ducked her head farther back into the shadows of the cubby as Jose turned in their direction. His gaze passed over Bill, who rested his chin against his chest, eyes closed, mouth hanging slack. Jose looked like he was getting tired of Miguel ordering him around. Lids heavy, he also looked like the alcohol they'd knocked back was catching up with him.

The sound of Jenny sobbing and pleading with Miguel filled the night and Megan clenched her fists. It could just as easily be her up there, and from what she'd heard so far, she was supposed to be the *prize* for Jose.

"Yeah, what?" Jose yelled.

"Put on some tunes. I want a little privacy for my lady and me up here." His laugh, laced with cruelty, rang through the quiet cove.

Jose fished his phone out of his pocket, his head down while he scanned the screen. It could be the best opening she'd get. She sprung up on her toes, ready to bolt.

"You want something romantic like ballads or boleros, or something—"

"I want something loud," Miguel yelled back.

"You don't have to do this," Jenny pleaded. "Please don't—"

She screamed as a loud crack filled the night. Bastard. He'd hit her again.

"Now." Miguel yelled.

Jose turned toward the galley door, looking through his playlists, and Megan took her shot, scrambling across the deck. She lowered herself over the starboard side of the speedboat, easing her legs into the water as quietly as possible. Bill held her upper arm, helping her descend more slowly into the water.

An old Rolling Stones number blared out of Jose's phone at maximum volume, the speaker tinny.

"Let me go," she whispered, sliding into the water. "Count to a hundred then distract him. I'll get to Dawn."

The music paused. Jose had heard her. Pressed against the side of the speedboat, her breath caught in her throat, she hoped he was too drunk to notice the small rocking of the boat. His shadow fell over the speedboat, over Bill's face and he called out, "Don't be greedy, Miguel. Remember you promised to share."

"Music," Miguel screamed back.

Jose put the music back on. Jenny's sobs filled the brief lulls between songs.

Staying as close to the hull as possible, Megan swam to the back of the speedboat. Diving below the surface, she swam under the stern of the boat, gauging the distance in her mind. The water was dark as coal, the warmth almost sticky against her skin. She wondered what lurked on the bottom beneath her.

She broke the surface a few feet off the port side of the Papa Joe, a narrow swath of light from the galley door glittering on the flat water. Careful to be quiet, she tilted her head back and took a breath.

Jose had begun tormenting Timothy, jabbing the toe of his shoe repeatedly into Timothy's ribs. Not getting enough of a reaction, he turned to Erik and planted a solid kick in his kidneys. Erik's grunt drowned out the music.

"What the hell is wrong with you?" Bill shouted. "Why don't you leave them alone?"

Jose's head swiveled like it was on a spit. He stepped to the edge of the stern and looked down into the speedboat. "Oh, he's awake." He laughed. "I thought we'd put you out for the night."

"What do you want with us?" Bill asked.

Megan swam quickly to the stern and clambered onto the platform. She popped her head up and caught Dawn's eye.

"That's none of your business," Jose said. He shrugged his shoulders and turned back. Megan dropped to her knees, out of sight. She held her breath. Water streamed off her body and dripped through the swimming platform into the mirror-like surface below. Each drip sounded like a hollow shot to her sensitive ears.

"Wait," Bill said, changing tact. "You have pretty good taste in music."

"Yeah I do."

"Man of taste," Bill said, stroking Jose's ego. "I like the old rock tunes too."

"Nobody will ever replace the Rolling Stones. Ever see them in concert?"

"No," Bill said, drawing out the word, a note of wonder in his voice. "Have you?"

Jose was warming up now, enjoying the attention. He turned to Bill and leaned his left shoulder against the ladder. "Saw a great concert with them on MTV," he said. "The one from Madison Square Garden in '69."

Megan wrapped her hands over the gunwale, pulled herself up over, and crawled quickly to Dawn, keeping an eye on Jose. Dawn raised her butt from the deck to give Megan more room to get to the rope.

Bill continued to stroke Jose's ego, confirming that he knew the concert and praising Jose's playlist.

Jose coughed and Megan hustled out of sight along the port side. Her breathing was ragged. How was it possible Jose couldn't hear her over the music? Up on the bow, Jenny's voice had taken on a pitiful, begging quality that tore at her heart. Keeping an eye on Dawn, she edged back to her side when Dawn indicated all was clear.

The Captain's hands were mostly loose, she'd obviously been working the rope, but the second line held her tight to the cleat. Megan's hands shook so badly her fingers fumbled at the rope. Frustrated, terrified Jose would turn at any second, she swore under her breath.

"Focus," Dawn said, so quietly Megan wasn't sure she'd heard her. She looked up at her, her gaze steady. "You can do this."

Megan held Dawn's gaze and nodded. She gulped in a breath, tamped her fear down, and quickly unraveled the two half hitches from the cleat. Then she nimbly stepped away as Jose turned his head toward them.

CHAPTER THIRTY-FIVE

Jose turned away from Bill in the speedboat and swung toward Dawn. She held her hands still behind her back, ignoring the tingling sensation in her wrists and resisting the urge to straighten her back now that she was loose. The muscles along her spine and shoulders screamed for release. He cocked his head, piercing her with a look and stalked across the deck closing the distance between them.

"Wait," Bill called out, "I need something to drink."

"Shut up," Jose said over his shoulder.

To Dawn's left, Megan edged farther up the port side, her back flat against the galley cabin.

Jose reached out and ran a finger down along the side of Dawn's face. She kept her features still and met his eyes. With the pad of his thumb, he traced the outline of her lower lip and licked his in an exaggerated way. In her peripheral vision, Dawn saw Timothy roll his weight forward, ready to pounce.

If Jose leaned six inches closer, Megan would be within his sight. She couldn't risk a glance in her direction to warn her. The rancid undertones of stale beer and tobacco in Jose's breath tripped her gag reflex. She swallowed hard and tried not to blink, determined to keep his focus on her.

"You're right pretty, too," he said, a grin splitting his face. His teeth were yellow, his right incisor capped with ugly silver metal. "I think Miguel won't mind if I play with you a while. He's busy up front in any case."

"Jose," Miguel yelled.

"Damn man has eyes in the back of his head," Jose said, jumping back from her. Dawn expelled a sigh of relief and caught Timothy's eye. Timothy settled back on the deck and lowered his head.

Miguel rounded the corner by the ladder. He glanced down into the speedboat. "That idiot is still out of it," he said to Jose. Stepping down onto the aft deck he waved a phone in his hand. "Check this out, her phone fell out of her back pocket while I was trying to get her shorts off."

"You're just now getting her shorts off? You mean she's still freaking dressed?"

A dark cloud stormed over Miguel's features. "What's it to you?"

Jose put his hands on his hips. "I'm waiting, is what it is to me. I thought you had her a long time ago."

"I'm in no rush," Miguel said, his gaze dropping to the screen in his hands.

"What's with all the crying and sobbing up there then?"

Miguel grunted. "You know me, Jose, I'm like a cat with a mouse. I enjoy the anticipation. Girl is scared shitless. It's a blast. She's putting on a real performance. But I know how we can ramp it up even more." He laughed cruelly.

Dawn's stomach twisted and it took all she had in her to not lunge at Miguel. At least he hadn't assaulted Jenny. Yet. She slanted a look up the port side. Megan crouched by the wheelhouse door and cocked her head toward the bow in question. Dawn inched her head to the side. It was too soon, too risky.

They needed to wait. Megan tipped her chin and stayed where she was.

"Check this out," Miguel said, throwing an arm around Jose's shoulder and drawing him closer. "The little Jenny cupcake is a model. Here's a bunch of photos of her." He swiped the screen, the two of them grunting appreciatively.

Timothy caught Dawn's eye and she shook her head. Wait, she mouthed.

Jose took the phone to look at something more closely and Miguel grabbed it back. "That's not the best part," he said. "Look at all her followers on Instagram. Over half a million. Know what I'm thinking?"

"What?"

"She's obviously an exhibitionist. Let's give her a chance to really entertain her followers." He barked out a laugh and turned away. "Too bad you guys can't be in on this," he said, his gaze sweeping over them. "Jose, find a strip song."

"Strip song?"

"Yeah, something strippers use. You know, like... the song from that movie, Nine and a Half Weeks. What was that?"

Jose frowned and started typing on his phone. "Leave Your Hat On."

Miguel turned away and started back toward the bow. "Let's see if our cupcake here can do it as well as Kim Basinger. I'm back," he said to Jenny, stretching out the words. "We're gonna have a little fun now darling and you can give us a different kind of performance. Stand up."

"Nobody do nothing." Jose scowled at them then followed Miguel to the bow.

Dawn scooted across the deck on her butt and untied Timothy. "Get Erik loose," she said.

She had a clear sightline through the galley and wheelhouse to the bow. Jenny stood, her hands tied in front. Her top had been removed, she was naked to the waist. Her shorts were unbuttoned and slung low on her hips, a bit of lace peeking out through the top of the zipper. Her face was tear stained, her eyes puffy and wild with fear.

"Let's do some video, a live feed to your followers," Miguel said.

Jenny shook her head. "No," she choked out. "I won't."

"You will or I'll throw you overboard. Or worse." Miguel turned to Jose. "Let's set the stage. There must be a spotlight inside."

Dawn shifted to the port side, out of the open doorway, and caught Megan sliding down the port side, away from the wheelhouse door. Dawn put her finger to her lips and her other hand up, palm open. Then Dawn crept back to the galley doorway.

Come on, find the spotlight. With the light in their eyes, the men would be night blind. Another advantage in her favor.

Thirty seconds later, Jose found the spotlight. He flipped it on, aiming it directly at Jenny. She blinked rapidly and cringed under the light, squeezing her shoulders together to cover her breasts with her upper arms.

"Don't be shy now, cupcake," Miguel yelled. "Drop your arms."

"Screw you!"

Miguel drew his fist back. Jenny sobbed and relaxed her arms, exposing herself.

Music blasted into the night at full volume. Jose had found the PA system and plugged his phone into it. Joe Cocker's infamous raspy voice belted out the words into the night.

Returning to the front deck, Jose accepted the phone Miguel passed him and trained the camera on Jenny. Miguel gestured wildly, pantomiming a strip tease, while Jenny's face crumpled.

The only small blessing was the loud music drowned out Miguel's words.

CHAPTER THIRTY-SIX

Heart pounding, Dawn stepped away to the side, and waved to Megan, motioning her to return and join them. Timothy had released Erik and left him to work on the rope around the Howes. Mrs. Howe slept, slumped against her husband.

"We need a plan," she said, as Megan and Timothy gathered around her.

"There's three of us, I say we just rush them." Timothy bounced on his toes.

"There's four," Megan said. "Bill is awake, he can help. He's just faking sleep right now."

"Bill?" Dawn asked.

"The other student. In the speedboat," Megan said, jerking her chin in that direction.

Erik guided Mrs. Howe's limp body gently to the deck and Mr. Howe stood and joined the circle, shaking the kinks out of his legs and rubbing his arms where the rope had cut in.

"So there's..." Timothy pointed at each in turn. Dawn, Megan, himself, Erik, Mr. Howe and he waved toward the boat. "Six of us. Three on each man. We rush them. Right now."

Dawn shook her head. "No," she said firmly. "Miguel still has a gun."

Timothy jammed his hands on his hips, his face turning red. "Why are you calling the shots?"

"Because I'm the Captain," she said.

"Yeah, but..." He grabbed her arm and turned her away from the others. "Apparently, *you're* the reason we're here," he hissed. "I don't know why but you brought all this trouble down on us. Not so sure we should be following your orders."

Dawn's blood boiled. The others listened intently. She didn't give a damn. "They wouldn't have found us if you'd simply followed my orders from the start," she said.

Megan grabbed Dawn's arm. "We're losing time. They're streaming that video live."

"I know," Dawn said. "But my job is to keep everyone safe, not save her reputation. We'll only have one shot at this, so we need to be strategic about this."

Timothy opened his mouth and Dawn put her hand up to stop him. She stared him down. "We do it *my* way."

"Fine." He spat the word out, daggers in his eyes. "Do you at least have arms on board? I have a sidearm in my gear, but it's stowed forward."

"I do," she said. "And I can access it in the galley." She looked around at each of them in the circle. "Here's what we're going to do," she said, dropping her voice to a lower whisper. They all leaned closer to catch her words.

———

In the galley, Dawn stood on the bed and stretched until her fingers brushed the case she'd stashed the Glock in. She'd fixed it to the top of the cabinet with velcro. There was barely enough room for her to slide her hand into the small space and pull it out. She removed her weapon, quickly loaded it and shoved it in the waistband at her lower back. Creeping up the galley stairs, she edged into the wheelhouse, keeping her body low. At the wheel, she peeked up over the top. The song was coming to an end, again—Jose had set it up to play on a loop— and Miguel was clapping encouragement while Jose bounced from side to side, trying various video angles.

Satisfied the two men were occupied, she moved to the door of the wheelhouse and held the gun out to Megan. "You know how to fire this?"

Megan nodded. "What about you? You have another gun?"

"I'll be fine," Dawn said. "We'll go on my signal." From above came two soft raps on the top deck. Timothy's signal. He was ready. She squeezed Megan's forearm. "Good luck."

CHAPTER THIRTY-SEVEN

B ENT DOUBLE AT THE WAIST TO STAY BELOW THE WINDOW, Dawn moved to the starboard door of the wheelhouse and poked her head out to peek toward the bow. At that moment, Jose turned and stumbled down toward her. She swiveled in place. Megan stared at her. Dawn gestured for her to move back and quickly slid down the stairs into the forward cabin.

At the bottom of the stairs she hesitated. Go where? She spied a large pile of blankets on one of the bunks and dived beneath it. Above her the music boomed. Miguel's laughter was manic. Jose stumbled past the opening to the stairwell and her breath hitched in her throat. She burrowed further into the blankets.

From her hiding spot, her gaze fell on several duffel bags. Timothy said his weapon was down here, but in which bag? She tried to picture what he'd brought onboard with him, but couldn't remember. She weighed the risk of trying to find it against the time it would cost her to search for it.

"I don't see it," Jose yelled.

"It's right there," Miguel yelled back.

Jose shut down the music. The silence was overwhelming. Dawn's heart pounded in her ears, replacing the bass line.

"What are you doing?" Miguel called.

"Changing the music." Jose fumbled around, messing with the PA controls and cursing under his breath.

"No! We're not done yet. Put it back on." Behind Miguel's voice, Jenny whimpered.

Impatience surged through Dawn. They needed to act.

She surveyed the hatch. Could she pop up fast enough to throw Miguel off balance? If she did, would Megan and Timothy back her up? It was a dangerous gamble.

"I didn't find it yet." Jose banged around in the wheelhouse.

"Never mind about that now. Get back here. Now."

Jose stumbled out of the cabin, colliding with a wall on his way.

"Not right now, idiot! Put the music back on first."

Grumbling loudly, Jose returned to the wheelhouse and turned the music back on. Dawn held her breath. If Miguel called for more booze or Jose decided to use the head or go to the galley for any reason, they were done for.

She heard him leave the wheelhouse, heard his footfall across the deck over her head. How had he avoided seeing Timothy? There was nowhere to hide on the roof.

"Get back over here and get the camera going again," Miguel ordered.

Throwing the blankets off, Dawn scurried back to the wheelhouse and eased herself up until she could see through the window. The spotlight had given Miguel and Jose night blindness. Probably the only thing that had saved Timothy. At that moment, two small taps on the roof confirmed he was still there, still in place and ready to go.

"Dance tiny dancer," Miguel yelled. He whooped into the night, clapping along with the music. Tears streamed down Jenny's face, her lips white as she clamped them tightly together. Her upper body shuddered with her sobs. Her shorts had slipped lower on her hips, she gripped the material in front of her crotch with her fingers, the rope on her wrists so tight Dawn could see the red welts.

She itched to rush them but couldn't gamble with Jenny's life or the lives of the others. Taking a breath, she planted her feet, determined to wait until she was certain.

Miguel stepped forward and slapped at her hands. "Let go," he ordered. "The tease part of the show is over, now you're going to strip for your followers. Be sure to get this, Jose, get in here closer."

Jose hit a button on the phone and said to Miguel, "Stop using my name."

"Get over it," Miguel said. "How many Jose's are there in this world. Put the volume back on, I want cupcake's followers to hear her tears. Isn't that right, cupcake? I thought you enjoyed being an exhibitionist, wanted the world to know all of your secrets, follow all of your movements."

Jenny gulped and grasped at her shorts as she spread her legs to keep them from sliding farther down her hips. Miguel planted a sharp kick at her knee. A sickening crack echoed through the air. Jenny screamed and buckled over, retching.

"Tease time is over, I said. Stand up straight." Jenny straightened and the shorts inched down her slender hips, exposing a lacy peach-colored thong. Jose closed in. She turned her face away, wailing.

Dawn met Megan's eye, brought her hand down in a go signal and moved out along the starboard side, her feet padding quietly up along the deck. Megan matched her pace on the port side.

They cleared the wheelhouse, coming up along the forward cabin, and Dawn chanced a look to the top deck. Timothy crouched, ready to jump.

Dawn exchanged a look with Megan and waved her forward.

They quickened their steps until they were less than two yards behind the men. Jenny, blinded by the spotlight, squinted as she tried to focus. Dawn shook her head violently.

Too late. Jenny fixed her stare on them. Miguel caught the look and spun toward them, his hand already reaching for his gun.

He yelled and fired.

CHAPTER THIRTY-EIGHT

MIGUEL'S SHOT SAILED OVER MEGAN'S HEAD. GRIPPING THE Glock in both hands to steady herself, Megan fired back. Her shot went wide and hit Jenny. Jenny screamed as blood blossomed at the top of her right arm.

Dawn hurled her weight toward Miguel. He sidestepped her and she collided with his shoulder. Behind her, Timothy landed with a thud and rushed forward. There was a whoosh close to her ear as he slashed through the air. His blade sliced Miguel's wrist. Yelping, Miguel dropped his gun. It bounced and skittered across the deck.

Miguel cursed. When he leaned forward to stop the blood gushing from his hand, Dawn spotted Jenny over his shoulder. As if in slow motion, Jenny's hooded eyes looked to the blood running freely from her shoulder, down her chest, over her belly. Perched on the bow of the boat, she swayed and her lids fluttered wildly, then she fainted, lost her balance and tumbled overboard. Her body bounced against the anchor line, her thigh sliding several inches along the taut rope, before she slid head first into the dark water below.

Before Dawn could open her mouth, Miguel wrapped his

good arm around her, gripping her to him in a tight embrace. She twisted her body, breaking his hold on her, stepped back and struck him hard, with an upper cut to the chin. His pupils widened and a low guttural sound escaped him.

Jose tackled Timothy, the two men falling to the deck. Timothy's knife clattered to the deck.

"Dawn," Megan cried.

"Go," Dawn yelled.

"Here, the gun!" Dawn turned to see Megan throw the gun in her direction. She jumped to reach it but it flew over her head and into the ocean.

There was a splash as Megan went over the side after Jenny.

Dawn calculated the distance to Miguel's firearm.

Miguel charged her and she ducked out of his way at the last second. She grabbed his upper arm as he passed her, used his own forward movement to propel him face first onto the deck. He cursed as his body slammed into the unforgiving wood.

Beyond him, Timothy scrambled to his feet and caught her eye. In that split second, Jose found his opening and sped forward, grabbed Timothy's legs and threw him off balance. Timothy teetered on the deck, reached down and dug his hands into Jose's neck. Dawn watched in horror as Timothy fell backwards, off the bow toward the water, taking Jose with him.

Dawn lunged toward the gun laying on the deck. Miguel scrambled forward and grabbed her ankle, his fingers clamped into her tendons. With her free leg, she kicked toward his face. He pulled her ankle forward at the same time and threw her off her feet. She landed hard on her back, the wind knocked out of her as her shoulder cracked against the corner of the forward hatch.

Miguel scrambled up her body until he straddled her hips. His mouth twisted in a cruel grin. He reached for her neck, his wrist dripping blood. "You're a piece of work," he sneered. "But now we can say good-bye."

Dawn braced her legs, lifted her butt off the deck, and dislodged Miguel. She flipped him off her hips. He cursed and hissed like a brawling cat. She ignored the pain shooting through her right arm and shoulder. Threw herself on top of him. Grappling, they rolled to the edge of the deck.

Below her, splashing water was punctuated by grunts and yells as Timothy struggled with Jose.

She spotted Miguel's gun. Another few inches and she could reach for it. She strained forward, her fingers stretching. Grasping it, she pulled it toward her. Miguel sunk his teeth into her shoulder. She screamed and dropped the weapon. It bounced on the deck, skittered to the opening by the cleat and slid over the side into the water.

She rolled back toward him and slammed her fist into his face. Blood gushed out his nose and his eyes opened wide, surprised at the force of her punch. He spit a stream of blood at her. Pupils darkened, his features screwed into a crazed look. Yelling, he pushed off the deck, jumped on her chest and reached for her neck.

Dawn's ears started to ring and her vision blurred like someone had dropped a gauze curtain in front of her face and she was looking through a fog. For a second, her world became larger, she heard everything around them in distinct detail. Timothy thrashing in the water with Jose, Megan somewhere off the port side struggling with Jenny, the purr of the outboard as the others made their escape. Then her world narrowed and everything went still. Her breaths came slow and measured. Would this be the moment she would join her dead brother?

She heard her brother's voice. "Help me, Dawn." Around her, the patrons of the seedy dockside bar clapped and whooped as three large bikers hammered her brother after he'd tried to hustle them at pool. She watched, her vision blurry, as one of them threw him onto the table, and another slammed a cue repeatedly over his lower back until the cue broke, one end flying through the air as several bystanders ducked to avoid it.

"Isn't that your brother?" The bartender picked up her empty bottle and swiped the moisture from the bar with a dirty rag. "You're not gonna do anything?"

"Aren't you? Hell, it's your bar." She rapped the bar with her knuckles.

"I think you've had enough," the bartender said.

"Never enough. Another beer. Bourbon back.

"Dawn," her brother yelled again. She turned her head, now it looked like there were two of him. The bodies of the men working on him shifted and blurred until the whole scene resembled something out of a 3-D movie.

She'd warned him a thousand times to be more aware of who he hustled. She hadn't thrown a punch since she'd left boxing and she wasn't about to now. He wanted to play with fire, he'd have to live with the consequences.

Except he didn't. She did.

The next thing she remembered was the ambulance, her parent's shock, the side glances she'd received at the funeral, standing hungover and peeking through slits in her eyes as the unforgiving sun beat down on them at his graveside. It should have been raining. Ominous dark clouds should have been rolling in over the horizon. Thunder, lightning even. Large over-sized black umbrellas gathered around the fresh dirt and the hole in the ground. That's how it happened in the movies. Who the hell buries their baby brother under clear blue skies? It wasn't right.

At the reception at her family home after, her uncle met her at the door, explained, for her parent's sake, she wasn't to attend. Not attend her own brother's funeral reception?

She'd crawled back into a bottle and stayed there until the day she'd crawled partway out, sick to death of being sick to death. The day she'd met Joe Black. If she died now, Joe's death would go unpunished.

Not fighting back had been the death of her brother, but it wouldn't be the death of her. This time, she was fighting back.

Miguel grunted, shocking her back to the present, his thumbs pressed into her windpipe, squeezing the life force out of her. She braced herself, jutted her hips into the air and brought her arm up against his elbow. His grip loosened. Screaming, fueled by regret and loss, she flipped him and straddled his chest. She punched him, repeatedly, her arms working in tandem. A machine. Relentless.

She pummeled him until his face was busted and his mouth went slack and his eyes rolled up into his head and went blank. Until he stopped making noise. When his lids slid over his eyeballs like the lid slamming on her brother's coffin, she took a breath and slumped, exhausted, on the prone, limp bulk of the man beneath her.

CHAPTER THIRTY-NINE

"Dawn, I need help." Timothy's voice brought her to her feet. She looked at Miguel. He was down for the count. Blood streamed from his mouth, nose and ears. His face resembled a rotting cantaloupe. She reached for the bow line to tie his wrist.

"Now, Dawn!" The urgency in Timothy's voice decided for her. Miguel wasn't going anywhere.

Running to the starboard, she scanned the water for him. Having the spotlight in her face for so long had made her night blind. "Where are you?" She listened for the splashes and moved toward the stern.

"Just below the galley," he said, his breath labored. "Jose is unconscious, I need help getting him to the platform."

Grabbing a boat hook from below the aft deck, she stepped up onto the stern. "Wait, I need better light." In the galley, she grabbed a flashlight from a drawer. She shined the light on the stern and Timothy pulled one arm toward it, his other arm wrapped around Jose's chest.

With the hook, Dawn got hold of Jose's belt and helped Timothy guide him to the platform. Once he grabbed on, she leaped down and pulled, while Timothy pushed, until they were able to roll his dead weight onto the platform. "Good work," she said. "I would have let him drown."

Timothy dragged in air in jagged spurts. He gripped the edge of the platform, his shoulders heaving. "Really?"

She shrugged. Probably not. She wanted to hand them over to the authorities.

"Miguel?" Timothy wretched and coughed up water.

"Out cold. Did you see Jenny and Megan?"

From above, Dawn grabbed one of the loose lines that had been used to tie them earlier. She wound it around Jose's wrists and tied him off tightly to the platform, wrapping it around his legs and chest to keep him from rolling off into the water.

"I could hear them. Want me to go after them?"

"Can you?" Extending a hand, she helped Timothy out of the water and up onto the deck. He collapsed in the corner, chest heaving.

"I need a minute."

"I'll secure Miguel." She grabbed another piece of rope and made her way to the bow. After securing Miguel's hands in front of him, and then tightly to a cleat, she returned to the stern.

Timothy hung over the side, spitting up sea water. Between his coughing spurts, the sound of splashing water reached her.

"Megan," she said. She ran through the galley to the wheelhouse and swung the spotlight over the water toward the shore, searching for Megan and Jenny.

Timothy came in through the starboard door. "Anything?"

"I hear them, but I can't find them." She trained the light in careful arcs in a back and forth pattern, moving closer to shore with each pass.

"There." Timothy pointed to a splashing motion where Megan was working hard with one arm, pulling toward shore.

"She'll be exhausted. We're going to lose them both. I'll go, you stay here and watch the men." Dawn stripped down to her swimsuit, throwing her shirt and shorts onto the wheelhouse bench. "Keep the light on them, so I can find my way," she said. She moved to the port door and the light shining on the water faded to black.

She turned back to Timothy. "I said—"

"I didn't touch anything," he said. Switches clicked as he switched the spotlight off then on again. More clicks as he tried other switches. "The battery is dead."

"Impossible." She crossed the wheelhouse to his side.

"Well, the spotlight and music have been blaring for while..."

"Still," she said. "Damn it, I need to get out there. Grab the flashlight from the stern and try to guide me with that."

"I can start the generator for the lights, put the trickle charger on the battery," Timothy said. "Or we can start the engine."

"No time. Those women could drown."

As she stepped out the port door and made her way down along the side, moving as quickly as possible in the blackness, something else in the night drowned out the splashing of the water toward shore.

CHAPTER FORTY

THE SOUND OF AN OUTBOARD MOTOR MOVING TOWARD THEM through the inky blackness droned across the water.

"Erik," she said. "They must have been close enough to see or hear what happened here and they're on their way back. Good timing." She stared into the dark, and Timothy came up alongside her. "We'll wait for them," she said. "We'll get to Megan and Jenny faster with the boat."

The boat came closer, the running lights visible as the small craft closed the distance between them.

"That's not Erik," Timothy said. He cocked his head. "That's an inboard."

"You can tell by the sound of the engine?"

"In time you will too. But right now, it could be anybody. Where's your gun?"

"I gave it to Megan. It's gone."

"Miguel's gun?"

"Also overboard. I thought you had a gun in your gear."

"I couldn't get to it and there's no time now. That's why I had the knife." His eyes narrowed. "And by the way, who the hell are these guys and why are they chasing you? All this time you're blaming it on me for giving those guys the coordinates, and you're the one they're looking for."

"They wouldn't have found us if..." Her words trailed away. Thanks in large part to Timothy, they were all still alive.

"I would have known not to if you hadn't been keeping everything on the down low. Don't you realize some secrets can be deadly? Who are these guys and what do they want with you?"

She stared at his battered face. "Look, you deserve an explanation, but there's no time." Through the night, the sound of the waves slapping against the bow reached them as the boat came closer.

Timothy's shoulders dropped slightly and he glanced off in the direction of the boat. "You have other arms on board?" he asked.

"I do. Hold them off and let them think you're here on your own." She went into the galley, then spun back toward Timothy. "Don't use any light. Let them work a little to find us."

Through the galley, through the wheelhouse and into the forward cabin, Dawn listened to the boat approaching. Down below, she ran her hands across the boards under the starboard porthole, looking for the one board that didn't rest flush with the others. Behind that board was the semi-automatic that Joe had stashed the day he'd died. She prayed there was ammo with it. With nothing else to pry it open, she used her fingernails. For the first time in her life, she wished she kept them long, but she did not. They were cut as short as possible, an old habit from her boxing days and the hours she'd wasted trying to learn a few chords on her brother's guitar.

A light flashed through the porthole as the engine stopped whining and gurgled down to a low drone. "There," came a man's voice.

"State your business," Timothy said.

She scratched at the wood, time running out, then pushed

hard on one end, pushing it in enough that it popped on the other end and gave her enough leverage to remove it. Reaching into the crevice behind it, she pulled the semi-automatic rifle out. It was heavy in her hands. A quick check confirmed that Joe had left it loaded.

Bracing on the bunk, she eased the front hatch open, inch by inch, careful to remain quiet. She peered out across the starboard bow and realized Miguel could easily be seen by the approaching boat.

The small boat was barely twenty feet off the starboard side now. "I'm a friend of Jenny's," came a man's voice.

Jenny?

"She told you where she was?" Timothy asked.

"No, we saw the video. What have you done with her, you bastard?" They shined a light in Timothy's face and Dawn popped up through the hatch and slithered her way to the window in front of the helm. She peeked around the corner. The two men in the boat stared up at Timothy.

Timothy held his hands up. "You've got it all wrong," he said. "We're also victims here."

"Where is she?" The second man held his arm out and cocked a small pistol. "Right now. Where is she?"

Dawn stepped out onto the starboard side, her weapon aimed at the boat. "Let's remain calm, gentleman," she said, her voice even.

"Stay where you are," yelled the man behind the wheel. He swung the spotlight in her direction. She turned her head slightly to the side but didn't take her eyes off them. When he saw the rifle, he told his friend to stand down.

She advanced down the side of the boat to the stern. "I'm the Captain. Tell me again how you found us."

The man behind the wheel did the talking, his words rushed. "We were fishing nearby. I follow Jenny, have for years. We picked up her Instagram and Twitter posts this afternoon, after she almost drowned." His forehead creased. "What kind of operation you running here anyway?"

"Keep talking," Dawn said. "Get to the point."

"We saw the posts later with the live video, with you... you... monsters forcing her to perform."

"She better be all right," yelled the second man.

Dawn put up her hand. "See the man on the back platform? He's one of them. We have the men who did this under control." She made a quick decision. "But Jenny still needs your help. Head for shore, you'll find a woman swimming toward the beach trying to save Jenny."

The man behind the wheel cocked his head. "You're not getting rid of us so easily," he said.

"She's telling the truth," Timothy said. "Jenny went overboard again. One of the other students is trying to get her to shore."

The two men glanced between themselves.

"Where do you think we'll go?" Dawn said. "Anyway, your boat could easily catch us."

The two men remained motionless.

She brought the rifle up again and pointed it at them.

"Go!" she yelled.

CHAPTER FORTY-ONE

The driver idled the small boat around the stern of the Papa Joe, shining the spotlight on Jose, still passed out and tied to the swimming platform. Then they headed directly to shore sweeping the spotlight from one end of the rocky beach to the other. At the far end of the beach, Dawn spotted the two women disappearing into the underbrush. Jenny was conscious, walking on her own, her arm slung over Megan's shoulder.

The small tree swayed, a piece of Megan's white T-shirt snagged on a branch. The limb swung wildly as the approaching boat grew closer to shore and Megan struggled to get free. Dawn wished there was a way to let them know the boat approaching was friendly, but she wouldn't be heard over the motor and her spotlight was dead.

Finally, the branch snapped back, with a bit of white material hanging from it. The motorboat had zeroed in on the same spot and idled just off shore, calling for Jenny.

"Jenny," Dawn called, "it's all right. Megan, come out." Her voice was lost on the night breeze, drowned out by the motor. Overhead, dark clouds skidded across the sky, obliterating even the light from the stars.

"What is that?" Timothy asked, turning toward the opening of the cove.

"What?" She looked in the direction he was pointing, the night so dark she couldn't tell where the sky ended and the water began.

"Another engine."

She bit her tongue. "Are you sure it's not their engine, the sound echoing back to us?"

"It's not. It's moving toward us and it's coming fast."

Dawn reached to the deck and picked up the semi-automatic. "Are you armed?"

Timothy held up the knife he'd retrieved from the forward deck.

"You have time to get your weapon from down below?"

"I looked. Someone stashed my bag somewhere." He cast a furtive glance toward shore and the other boat. "I wish there was a way to warn them."

The boat shined their light on the band of trees that laced the top of the rocks, on the spot where Megan and Jenny had disappeared. One of the men turned back toward the open water and killed both the motor and the spotlight.

"Are you heading back inside?" Timothy asked.

Dawn was already inside the galley door. "Same plan as before," she said, moving forward as quickly as possible. As she passed through the wheelhouse, a strong light hit the Papa Joe broadside.

"Papa Joe, this is the Coast Guard, answering your distress call."

Timothy raced up the side and stuck his head in the wheelhouse. "I guess Erik was able to get a call out. Good thinking, Captain." Timothy gave her a half salute and returned to the stern to take a line.

Dawn had sent Erik, Bill, and the Howes off in Miguel's

boat to keep them out of harm's way and to radio for help. She wondered where they were shored up.

"We almost didn't find you, it's so dark," one of the Coasties said.

"Battery is dead," Timothy said, catching the line and pulling the smaller boat alongside. "We haven't had much time to get things going again."

"Permission to board, Captain."

Dawn stepped down along the starboard side. "That would be me," she said. The man turned toward her and tipped his hat. "Permission granted," she said.

"Just what is going on here?" The first man stepped aboard. "Is everyone all right?"

Words tumbling, Timothy and Dawn started to bring the two men up to speed. As they talked, the senior officer looked over the stern at Jose's crumpled body tied to the platform, his expression pinched. "Go check on the other one," he said to his colleague who at once moved forward.

"He's in bad shape," the man yelled from the bow.

Timothy was mid-sentence when the man held up his hand. "We'll take your report later," he said. "For now, we need to get these men to shore. It looks like they'll both need medical attention."

"Some of our people also need medical attention," Dawn said.

The officer's eyes darted around. "Where are they?"

"They're—"

"Never mind," he said, waving his hand. "Unless they're dying in the next few minutes, we'll have to come back for them. We'll need your help getting these two men aboard our boat."

"Wait," Dawn said, annoyance eating at her. Her only experience with the Coast Guard had been with Captain Cutter, but these two were helping her to understand why Joe hated them so much. "One of our students almost drowned. She needs—"

"As soon as we're underway with these two, I'll call a chopper to get out to you. He can be here in under twenty minutes."

"Let's get Mmm... let's get the man at the bow first," the second Coastie said. Miguel was dead weight. The two men struggled as they carried him down along the side and got him onto their boat.

Dawn and Timothy untied Jose from the platform and lifted him to the gunwale of the other boat, where the Coastie pulled him aboard and laid him gently down on the deck. Seconds later, the pilot had the engine going.

"Where are you taking them?" Dawn asked.

"We'll let you know," he said.

"Give us a status," she said.

He cocked his head.

"An ETA for the helicopter." Her tone was clipped and she didn't give a damn.

He nodded abruptly and backed the boat away from them, then turned back toward the open water and raced away into the night, their running lights and masthead light cutting a path for them over the waves.

"That was odd," Timothy said.

"What the hell?" Dawn hauled herself back on deck from the platform. "Let's get the generator going so we receive that radio call when it comes in and we need some lights for when the chopper arrives. I want to see what's happening on shore."

CHAPTER FORTY-TWO

Timothy started the engine to charge the battery. Dawn flipped on the spotlight and shined the light on the shore. The two men were pacing the tree line at the top of the beach, calling repeatedly for Jenny.

Grabbing the microphone, Dawn turned on the PA. "Jenny, Megan, these men are friends. Come out and let them bring you back to the boat."

Moments later, the bush at the far end of the beach shook and Jenny and Megan stepped out. The two men rushed forward and supported Jenny between them. Her face was pale and she blinked under the bright light.

Megan hobbled along behind. Midway down the beach, she stumbled and crashed to the ground. Jenny's super fan rushed to her side and helped her up, supporting her weight with his arm under her shoulder. The four of them picked their way back to the boat. She kept the spotlight on them until they pushed off the beach.

Once the men had helped the women on board, Dawn grabbed blankets off the bed in the galley and wrapped them around the shoulders of both Jenny and Megan. Jenny still shook. Dawn guessed she was in shock.

"Hey Timothy," she said. "Can you switch the radio to the PA so we won't miss that call."

"Sure thing."

"And turn on some running lights," she called after him as he ducked through the galley.

Megan's limbs trembled violently, her skin raw and puckered. "Good work," Dawn said, rubbing Megan's arms briskly. "I think you might have a little hypothermia. I'll make you both something warm to drink."

The aft speaker popped overhead as Timothy plugged the radio into the system. The two men sat awkwardly on the bench, watching Jenny and Megan.

She turned to them, shook their hands and thanked them. "I can't believe you found us because of that video," she said.

"The guy streaming the video didn't disable location on his phone. It was easy really." The super fan shrugged. "I'm Gerry," he said, then pointed to his friend, "this is Andy."

"Very good timing guys and smart thinking on shore turning off the lights, but as it turned out it was the Coast Guard so it would have been safe."

"I didn't want to take any chances," Gerry said. "I thought the bad guys might have some friends show up."

"Well, it's not over until it's over," Dawn said, a small laugh she didn't feel escaping her lips. "They're taking them to the hospital now, and then they'll be handed over to the authorities and thrown in jail. We can't thank you guys enough."

"What about a drink," Timothy said, reaching over to shake both men's hands. They nodded and he pulled a cooler out from below the aft deck and passed them both beers.

"Maybe we should get the women to the hospital," Gerry offered. "I mean, like you said, we'll run faster than you will. We're happy to do it." He stood and his friend stood with him.

"Thanks, but the Coast Guard is sending a chopper. That's the call we're waiting for." Dawn glanced to the east where a purpling of the sky indicated sunrise was less than an hour away. "You're welcome to stay until dawn," she said, "so you don't have to run back in the dark."

The men exchanged a look, decided it was a good idea and sat back down.

She nodded to them before stepping into the galley to make tea. The stress of the last few hours poured out of her as she filled the kettle from the tap. It was the first moment she'd had to herself since it had all begun, her first opportunity to reflect and digest any of it.

And that's when it started again. Her jaw clenched and her muscles tightened as the little guy with the pickaxe tapped away at her gut to get her attention.

CHAPTER FORTY-THREE

With the crisis behind them and the women safe, she wondered why Erik, Bill and the Howes weren't back. They should have been monitoring the radio and come back to the Papa Joe when the Coast Guard arrived.

Had they run out of gas? Gone ashore? Encountered some other problem that prevented them from returning?

The hissing of the kettle drew her out of her thoughts and she splashed hot water into two cups and threw tea bags in. As the bags sunk into the hot liquid, she pulled down a third cup for herself. She'd prefer coffee, it had been a long night, but tea was easier and already made.

She took the drinks out to Megan and Jenny. Neither woman had improved in the few minutes she'd been gone. "Here, this might help," she said, passing them each a cup.

Jenny thanked her and returned her attention to Gerry, who was explaining how he could remove the videos from the account so no one else could see them. "A permanent removal," he said.

"Be sure to keep copies, and a record of it," Dawn said.

"I want it all gone," Jenny said.

"They'll need it for evidence, to charge them."

"Right." Gerry returned to his plan for getting the videos away from prying eyes.

Dawn put her arm around Megan's shoulder. Cold rippled off her in waves. "You saved Jenny's life."

Megan breathed sharply in through her nose. "I wasn't sure I'd make it." She dropped her voice. "She was dead weight at first, and halfway to shore she woke up and fought like a banshee."

"Drowning people panic."

"I thought she would take us both down. It was so dark, the only way I knew if we were above or below surface was whether I was breathing air or water." She coughed. "I took in my share of salt water."

"You're really strong," Dawn said with real admiration. She'd never had a true female friend and had never met anyone as grounded as Megan. Tightening her arm around her shoulder, she tried to transfer as much body warmth to her as possible. "You did an amazing job."

From behind them, came the sound of an engine. "Finally, Erik." She chuckled and glanced up at Timothy, who shook his head. "No, what?"

"It's not their boat."

"Oh, come on, you can't know that far away."

"And yet I do," he said. "It's not their boat."

Dawn sprang to her feet. "Everyone inside," she said. "You two," she said, looking to Gerry and Andy, "help the women inside. Timothy, you're with me." She raced ahead through the galley with Timothy on her heels. In the wheelhouse, she turned to him and threw up her hands. "Now what?"

He mirrored her gesture. "I don't know. Maybe Miguel's men coming for him." His hand reached for his knife. "Same plan as before?"

"Yes," she said, starting to descend the forward cabin stairs, "but kill the PA. And the lights. The chopper should be here any minute. Let's try to hold them off."

She went forward, stuck her head out the hatch and watched the boat speed toward them, its running lights coming closer by the second. In the galley, Jenny sobbed quietly while Gerry tried to comfort her.

Adrenalin pumped through Dawn's body and she bounced on the bed, preparing herself to spring through the hatch when they came alongside. The super fan's speedboat was along the starboard, so they'd have to come along the port.

When the boat came within twenty feet, they slowed the engines and their wake lifted their stern and rolled toward the Papa Joe. They floated in on the wave.

"Papa Joe, this is the Coast Guard. Prepare for us to come alongside."

Like hell. She waited while they idled around the stern and came up along the port side. A man stood on the stern ready to throw a line.

"Papa Joe, we're responding to your distress call. If no one greets us, we're going to board your vessel."

Dawn slid out of the hatch and edged along the forward cabin to the corner of the wheelhouse, this time looking down along the port side. The boat flew Coast Guard insignia. Clever. It almost looked authentic.

She stepped into their light with the semi-automatic rifle aimed at the man behind the helm. "You're not boarding my boat," she said.

"Ma'am, it's the Coast Guard. I need you to stand down."

Ma'am? Since when had she graduated to ma'am?

"Sure it is," she said. "The Coast Guard was already here and their chopper is on the way. Why would they send another boat?" She laughed and swung the business end of the rifle toward the man holding the stern line. Timothy stepped up on the aft deck into her sight line.

"No," the man said firmly. "We're responding to your distress call. We were the nearest vessel."

Dawn bit her lip, the muscles in her body tense as the inside of a golf ball. "Show me some identification."

The Captain stepped partway out the door and jabbed a finger at the insignia on his shirt and his hat.

"Yeah, good costume Captain. I need something more."

The man threw his hands up, then reached into his back pocket and pulled out his wallet. He flipped it open and extended it toward Dawn. It also looked authentic.

Dawn shook her head. "I'm not letting you board."

"Look, I understand you're in a stressful situation here. Is anyone's life in immediate danger?"

Timothy caught Dawn's eye and raised his brow in question.

"Get on the radio, then," Dawn said. "Have the Coast Guard confirm you're who you say you are."

"Fine." The Captain grabbed his microphone to make the call. Dawn held up her hand.

"Timothy, get inside and make sure he's on the right frequency."

Timothy sprinted through the galley and a few seconds later confirmed they were good to go.

"Go ahead," Dawn said, tipping her chin at the so-called Captain.

The man made the call and the response came back quickly. "Papa Joe, this is Captain Cutter. Captain Wayne Cutter. Dawn, pick up please."

CHAPTER FORTY-FOUR

DAWN BACKED ACROSS THE FRONT OF THE WHEELHOUSE, NOT lowering her weapon. With one hand, she reached toward the window and Timothy passed her the microphone.

"Wayne?"

"Dawn, what is going on over there? We received a distress call that you'd been boarded by pirates. Are you all right? Is anyone injured?"

She stared at the mic in her hand and looked up at Timothy slack-jawed. If this was the Coast Guard, then who had taken Miguel and Jose?

"Dawn?" Wayne's voice came through the radio. "Are you okay?"

"Yes, Captain," she said. "Do you have a chopper coming out for us?"

"Chopper? If you need it, yes. We'll let the crew assess what you need first. Have my men arrived?"

"They're just about to board," she said, tipping her chin toward the Captain who was watching her through his wheelhouse door.

"Captain Birch, I want a full report once you assess the situation."

"Roger that, Captain Cutter. Over and out."

Behind her, Dawn heard the high-pitched whine of a motor and turned to see a speedboat with four people aboard speeding toward them through the early morning light. She didn't need the binoculars to confirm it would be Erik and the others.

"Timothy, take care of Erik's boat when they get here," she said. She moved forward to greet Captain Birch as he stepped through his wheelhouse door and through hers. She extended her hand. "Sorry for the extra precautions. We were boarded by the so-called Coast Guard less than an hour ago."

His brows pinched together. "What?"

"Yeah, two men in a small boat. Said they were Coast Guard, responding to our call. They took the two men we were holding."

Emotion stormed across his face. "Give me a complete description of the two men and the boat." Once she'd run down everything she could remember, he said, "Give me a minute, would you?" and returned to his radio to make a call.

There was a lot of activity in the galley and Dawn stuck her head in at the top of the stairs. A medic was looking over Jenny. A strip thermometer was plastered to Megan's forehead.

She passed through to the aft. Gerry and Andy sat on the side bench. "The Coast Guard asked us to stick around a little longer to give a statement," Gerry said.

"Good. You guys were a huge help." Her gaze swung to the boat drifting up to the stern. Timothy guided them and Erik nosed the bow in until Timothy told him to kill the engine. Erik and Bill sat in the front seats, with the Howes huddled together in the back. All four looked wiped out. And cold.

"I'm glad you guys made it back," she said. They all started talking at once. She held up her palm. "Easy," she said. "First things first. Let's get you aboard and warmed up." Bill helped the Howes, Mrs. Howe first, step across the bow and onto the deck. She was rumpled, her cheeks pink and her eyes droopy, but otherwise unharmed. Mr. Howe squared his shoulders and tried to look dignified, despite the obvious exhaustion weighing on him. Bill boarded next, his hand clammy and cold in Dawn's, followed by Erik.

"Good job, Erik," Dawn said, shaking his hand as he stepped onto the deck. "We couldn't have done it without you."

He nodded, eyes sparkling. "So the Coast Guard got them? Where are they? Already in the hold on their ship? I can't wait to see them taken to jail."

Dawn's chest tightened. "I'm afraid not."

"They got away?" He looked around. "How? We have their boat. And who are these other guys?" he asked, spying the two super fans.

Captain Birch stepped into the group. "Dawn, can you ask all your passengers to assemble here, please?"

Dawn looked at Timothy. "I'll get them," he said.

"I've issued an alert," the Captain said. "The sun is almost up so we should be able to find them."

She nodded but she wasn't hopeful. For one, they'd had a head start. Plus, there were a lot of places they could hide. "Give me a minute, would you?" Running to the forward cabin, she grabbed more blankets and brought them aft for the Howes, Bill, and Erik.

The sun inched over the horizon as Jenny and Megan squeezed onto the back deck to join them.

It concerned her that two complete strangers, Gerry and Andy, would hear all the details of the night. She had liability forms signed by the students, but not by Gerry and Andy and given how online media savvy Gerry was, she was reluctant to go into detail with them there. She would have to pull the Captain aside before they got into things.

"We can take statements here," Captain Birch said, putting

up his finger when Dawn stepped forward, "shouldn't take more than an hour or so. Or," he cast an eye around the group, "we can get you back to shore and do statements a bit later today. Once you've had a chance to rest, eat, get warmed up."

A chorus of agreement sprang from the group. "Okay, here's the plan then." He spent the next few minutes outlining how the morning would roll out. Before he stepped back on his own vessel, he pulled Dawn to the side.

"I'll have one of my men pilot the men's speedboat back," he said. "As for the two men who joined you later—Jenny's fans? —I'm going to interview them privately. They weren't party to most of what went on here tonight so there's no point in involving them more."

"Thank you, Captain," Dawn said. "What about Jenny and Megan? Will they ride back with you and the medic?"

"I think that's for the best. Medic says Jenny's gunshot wound is surface, but we'll take them both to Emergency. Two of the men are pretty beat up. And you," he said, scrunching his face as he took in the cuts and bruises to her face and arm. "Medic said you're fine for now but you should all get medical attention later today."

"I'm fine," she said.

"If only for ibuprofen." He tipped his hat back and scratched at his scalp. That small movement reminded her of Joe and for a second, she wondered if his spirit had somehow helped her through this, somehow kept them all safe.

"I want you to get the rest of these folks straight back to the marina and then cut them loose to eat, shower, rest. There's a good hotel at the south end, you know it? It's an easy walk. Send them all there. We'll start interviews at fifteen hundred hours. That's three o'clock."

Dawn nodded. "I know."

"I'll want you present for all of it," he said, looking down his long straight nose at her. "As Captain of the Papa Joe, Cutter wants you involved every step of the way. I haven't had a chance to get to know him yet, but sounds like you've got a good friend in that man."

He turned away, then back again. "The minute we have eyes on the imposters and those two thugs they rescued, I'll be in touch."

"Thanks, Captain Birch," Dawn said as he returned to his own boat.

He waved his hand over his right shoulder. "Get some rest, Captain."

CHAPTER FORTY-FIVE

DAWN STOOD BESIDE A HEAP OF DISCARDED BLANKETS ON THE deck. Jenny stepped aboard the Coast Guard vessel, assisted by the medic. He turned and extended his hand to Megan.

"It's overkill," Megan said, turning to face Dawn. "I don't need the hospital."

Dawn put a hand on her arm and chuckled. "Your lips are still blue. Go to the hospital. I'll see you this afternoon at the interview."

"You'll be there?"

Nodding, Dawn said, "I will. We can talk more then."

Megan leaned forward, and Dawn instinctively shifted to the side before realizing the woman was trying to hug her. "Old habit," Dawn said, feeling silly, and then she let Megan wrap her arms around her and give her a squeeze.

Dawn clapped her on the back. "Good job," she said for what felt like the hundredth time. It was inadequate and she knew it but she didn't know how to deal with her friendly feelings for Megan. She hadn't had a friend of the female persuasion since grade school. Well, she had time to sort it out and she would see her again at the interviews.

As the Coast Guard pulled away, Gerry and Andy boarded their boat and fired up the motor. Miguel's boat was already gone, on its way to the Coast Guard yard piloted by one of the other officers. She and Timothy said goodbye to the two men. She'd see them later too. Captain Birch had already spoken to them about the sensitive nature of the investigation and the need for them to hold everything in confidence. Although she itched to say something about that including social media, she bit her tongue, gave them a big wave and thanked them for their help.

As she took in the others still sitting on the stern, her heart fell. What a pitiful looking bunch. She smiled at Timothy. "Could you get some coffee going?"

His gaze swept the four remaining students and his face softened. "Sure." He grabbed an armload of the discarded blankets on the deck and went inside. A moment later, the clattering of the percolator and running water drifted out from the galley.

Jamming her hands in her pockets, Dawn sat on the bench beside Erik. "You look tired," she said, quietly.

"It was a long night," he said, passing his hand over his head. He slanted her a look. "Are you going to bring us up to speed with everything that went on while we were out there?" He waved a hand to the open water. "I mean, we've heard some of it but not all the details."

Dawn breathed in. All eyes were on her. Bill's face in the morning light was unfamiliar to her. She'd barely seen him. The Howes snuggled together under a blanket. "I'm not sure I can. What I mean is, I don't want to add extra information before you have your interviews with the Coast Guard."

"I don't see why they need to talk to us, dear," Mrs. Howe said. "We weren't even here."

"Well, you were here for part of it," Dawn said. "They need a complete picture of everything that happened and I'm sure they'll want to know how things went when you were gone in the speedboat."

"I can fill you in on that right now," Erik said.

"No." Dawn shook her head. She looked at each of them in turn. "It will all come out this afternoon. The important thing," she looked back at Erik, "is that you got everyone to safety and called for help." He nodded, his mouth tight. "Good job," she said. There it was, that feeling of inadequacy again. Surely she could express herself better than that.

"Coffee?" Timothy stepped onto the back deck with a fistful of mugs and passed them around. He returned with the percolator and poured coffee.

Dawn sipped hers, the hot liquid like fire in her belly, and nodded for Timothy to join them.

"I meant what I said," she started.

"We wanted to stay here to help," Erik said.

"I know, but the smartest thing was to keep you safe and away from here so you could call for help. Thanks to you and Bill that happened. Where did you shore up for the night?"

Erik gave her a half grin. "I thought you didn't want to discuss the details?"

She laughed and clinked his mug with hers. "Fair enough." Looking at each of them in turn, she said, "You did great."

"But those men got away, is that right?" Mrs. Howe raised her head from her husband's shoulder and sat up straight. "So, the things they did to Jenny... " Her voice choked with emotion and she swiped a tear from her eye. "Those assholes won't have to pay for that?" The edge in her voice surprised Dawn.

"They'll pay," Timothy said. He caught Dawn's eye. "Dawn almost killed Miguel. And," he paused for effect, "Jose wasn't in much better shape."

"But you let them get away," Mr. Howe said, jumping into the conversation, his tone accusatory.

Eyes narrowed, Timothy spoke evenly. "After we disarmed

them, and removed the harm from Jenny, we turned them over to the Coast Guard. Is that what you meant to say?"

Mr. Howe's bushy brows inched together, dominating his face. "The fake Coast Guard, as it turns out."

"As it turns out," Timothy repeated Mr. Howe's words. "There's no way we could have known it at the time. Those men were smart and well prepared. No way we could have seen that coming."

"Even if they were hurt," Mrs. Howe said, "that's not enough. They won't be brought to justice."

"We don't know that yet," Dawn said. "Look, I understand we're all disappointed that the men escaped. But they won't get away with what they did. The Coast Guard has alerts out for them and they could be caught this morning." They looked so dejected, she felt obligated to hold out some hope to them, but she didn't believe it herself. The chances of them being caught on open water with such a head start were slim.

Everyone was subdued for several minutes, the mood somber.

Bill shifted in his seat, then he said, "You don't believe that."

"I promise you, one way or another, they'll pay. There's more than one kind of justice." Dawn stared down Bill then met each of their eyes in turn, putting an end to the conversation.

Nursing the dregs of her coffee, she leaned back, watching the last of the pink disappear from the horizon as the sun inched higher in a bright blue sky. There was not a breath of wind, the ocean smooth as an egg shell. It would be a beautiful day to cruise.

She got up and nodded to Timothy, ready to pull anchor and head back in. Hard to believe they'd been gone barely twenty-four hours.

CHAPTER FORTY-SIX

DAWN GAVE THE WHEEL TO TIMOTHY TO FINESSE INTO THE slip and went out on deck to help Erik and Bill with the lines. The Howes were busy packing up their belongings in the galley. She'd also put Mrs. Howe in charge of collecting Jenny and Megan's things.

All was quiet when they cruised into the harbor, nobody waiting for them at the dock. She wasn't sure what she'd been expecting, but after the last few hours, the calm seemed surreal.

She tossed the stern line down to Bill then walked forward and sent the bow line sailing over to Erik. Returning mid-ship, she jumped down onto the dock and checked their knots. They'd both learned a lot in a short period of time. On one level, perhaps the course had been a success.

"Timothy," she yelled up. He stuck his head out the wheelhouse door. "Once everything is stowed, let's have everyone gather on the pier."

Twenty minutes later, the bedraggled group of students circled around her. She shifted to get her face out of the direct sun and cleared her throat.

"Before you leave, there's a couple of things," she said.

"First, as Captain Birch outlined earlier, you'll each be interviewed this afternoon starting at 3 p.m. I need you all in the lobby of the hotel, ready to go, fifteen minutes before that."

Mrs. Howe tugged on her husband's sleeve. He cleared his throat and said, "That's only six hours from now. We need more rest than a handful of hours."

Dawn put her hand up. "Not my schedule," she said. "Let's just get through this the best that we can. Timothy radioed ahead and the hotel has rooms ready for all of you. Order room service, have a shower, take a nap. We'll see you at 2:45. Clear?" She looked around the group and they all nodded.

"Erik, you should probably go to the hospital and have your nose looked at. Timothy, you too." Both men shook their heads, declining her suggestion.

"The other thing... " She swallowed. She knew this would be hard but it was the right thing to do. "We're refunding your course fees."

"Damn straight," Bill said. Dawn was glad she hadn't seen much of him because he definitely rubbed her the wrong way. Right now she wanted to cuff him across the mouth.

Timothy grunted. "What she means to say is, we're going to consider refunding a *portion* of your fees, once we have a chance to assess things. Isn't that correct, *Captain*?"

She avoided his eyes. "No, Timothy, it is not. I meant exactly what I said. Each of you will be reimbursed for your course fees. In full." The small group nodded and thanked her.

"Now if you can manage your own bags, I'd say pack up and head over to the hotel." She pointed to the sign on the corner of the six-story building to the south of the marina parking lot. "I'll see you in a few hours."

CHAPTER FORTY-SEVEN

"Have you lost your mind?" Timothy said.

She shushed him. "Keep your voice down." The students were mid-way down the dock and hadn't hit the shore yet.

Timothy bounced from the ball of one foot to the other, a move she was coming to know well. The minute Erik, who was in the lead, hit the shore, he exploded.

"Refund their money? We can't afford to do that," he said. "The whole point of you taking this charter for me was so I wouldn't lose the income."

She shrugged. "What do you want me to say Timothy? It's the right thing to do."

He sputtered. "Don't you know anything about business? They paid for a service and we provided it—"

"How do you figure that? They paid for a three-day course and they're back at the dock in twenty-four hours. They were put through hell. Don't you get that?"

"I get that," he said, his fists braced against his hips. "In case you hadn't noticed, I was there and also put through hell." He touched his upper arm which was badly bruised. His hands were cut and scratched. There was a large gash over his left eye, his right cheek swollen and turning purple. Jose hadn't gone down without a fight.

"I want you to go to Emergency later today. Or now," she said.

He shook his head. "No."

"You might have internal injuries," she said. "You were kicked pretty bad on the back deck."

His eyes narrowed. "Medical treatment costs *money*," he said.

"There's no way we can justify keeping their money."

"We can't even pay our operating costs," he said, the veins popping in his neck. "You put all that fuel on credit with the marina." His arm swung wildly toward shore. "How are you going to cover that? All those groceries? And liquor? All on my credit card." He poked his chest for emphasis.

Dawn cringed but held his stare. "I don't know, Timothy. Honestly, I don't have a solution and I'm as stressed about it as you are."

"You brought this on us," he said, getting in her personal space again. "You." He jabbed his finger at her. "What the hell was that all about? I deserve that explanation now."

She looked at his finger until he withdrew his hand. She sighed. "I suppose you do. But I'm not talking to you about it until you calm down a little. Can you do that?"

"Stop talking to me like I'm a child," he said, stomping his foot against the dock.

Dawn stifled her smile. "Fine. Stop acting like one." She arched her brow and met his eye until he took a breath and stepped back. "It's about when Joe died. Most of the story didn't go public, but I can fill you in on a lot of it, if you promise to keep it confidential." She couldn't, she was still a key witness and she couldn't tell him any of that. In fact, now that they were back two days earlier, the hearing was probably taking place right now, while she was wasting her time arguing with Timothy on the damn pier.

"Not a lot of it," he said, "*all* of it. And I thought Joe drowned."

"He did." She bit her lip and gazed out beyond the boat to the harbor beyond. It hurt her to think about it, to talk about it was even worse. And she hated feeling vulnerable. Especially around someone like Timothy.

"Then what?" He cocked his head, the muscles in his face relaxing, her sadness mirrored in his eyes.

She sucked in another breath. "The charter we took out that day, the diving charter, it went bad."

"In what way?"

"There was something else going on. Some treasure hunting, we think." She shrugged. "It's not really clear yet what the whole deal was, but —"

"But what? If you're going to tell me, tell me all of it."

"Would you shut up and let me finish what I was saying? Do you think it's easy for me to talk about this?" Her eyes filled with tears and she cursed her weakness as she swiped them away with the back of her hand. She looked at Timothy through a prism of moisture and rainbow hues.

He rolled back on his heels and tipped his chin, clearly shocked by her raw emotion.

"We were boarded by Cubans, friends of the guy who set up the charter. It got pretty ugly."

"Is that how you hurt your wrist?"

"Yeah. They had Joe and I tied up, and then," she paused and glanced off in the distance again, her voice breaking, "and then, before they took off, they threw Joe overboard."

Timothy's mouth hung open. "Joe's a strong swimmer. I don't understand."

"Joe *was* a strong swimmer," Dawn said. "His hands were tied. He didn't have a chance."

"You said he was tangled in a line and caught under water too long. That he took in took in too much water, and that's why he didn't make it. He was air lifted to the hospital." Timothy's words tumbled out of his mouth in a rush, one heaping on the next. "Dawn, none of what you're telling me makes sense."

"I know. The authorities put together a cover story. It's true that he was air lifted, and we thought he was going to make it." Sadness ripped through her. She remembered diving over the side and dragging him, unconscious, back to the surface. "Once the men left, I went overboard and brought him up. Turned out I was too late."

She jammed her hands in her pockets, shoulders hunched, wanting that to be the end of it.

"Are you saying this was somehow related?"

"It's possible."

"Those men were after you." He shook his head. Dawn could almost hear the crank of the rusty wheels turning in his head. He pursed his lips and squinted against the sun. "We'll refund half their course fees. Your half."

"We're going to refund it all, Timothy, every penny. Once this settles down, I'll figure out a way to cover our expenses so you won't be out of pocket."

A deep flush crept up Timothy's neck and into his face until she thought he might explode. "We all could have died out there."

She backed off, putting some physical space between them, and held her palms up. She had enough enemies, she couldn't afford to make another one. Though it galled her, she had to at least try to keep the peace with Timothy.

"I'm deeply sorry you were involved in what happened out there" she said, her regret genuine. "For what it's worth, I'd probably be dead if you hadn't been there."

Timothy brushed past her and stomped down the dock toward his own boat. He didn't turn as he threw his final words back over his shoulder.

"Maybe that would have been better."

CHAPTER FORTY-EIGHT

Dawn rummaged through her clothes, looking for the shirt with the fewest wrinkles. If she hurried, she could still make it to the court house in time for the hearing. Especially after last night, she wanted to hear for herself what Nico and Mark had to say. Even though Nico had helped her in the end, and Mark had been underwater for most of the time, they still had ties to Dylan and Felix, and for that she intended to see they were held accountable.

The lawyer had warned her to stay away but leaving hadn't protected her. She was done being ruled by fear.

She settled on a navy button down and pulled it on over a clean pair of jeans. Kicking her feet into her hiking sandals, she stepped into the head and dragged a brush through her hair. After a couple of minutes, she gave up, tossing the brush back into a basket. Dark circles blemished the skin under the eyes that stared back at her from the mirror. A jagged gash ran down her right cheek, one eyebrow was split open, her jaw was bruised, her lips swollen. She grimaced at her reflection and climbed up to the wheelhouse to find her phone. As she picked it up, it chirped.

Dawn, I heard about what happened. Don't even think about coming to the hearing. I'll be in touch with news later. Keep your head down.

She stared at the screen. Thomas Duncan, efficient as always. She read the message a second time. Her life, her call. She tucked the phone in her back pocket, closed up the wheelhouse and headed through the galley. The phone chirped again.

I'm going in now. You won't be here in time to see anything. Trust me to take care of this. Stay under the radar.

She glanced at the time. The courthouse was twenty minutes away. If she hurried, she might make it for the last few minutes, at least to get a glimpse of Nico and Mark and whoever came out to support them.

The phone chirped a third time.

It's what Joe would have wanted.

And there it was. The curse of a lawyer who was also your mentor's friend. In the grave and somehow Joe was still managing to look out for her.

She returned to her berth, lay down fully dressed and stared at the ceiling, the sunlight streaming in through the hatch overhead.

Five more hours until the interviews. She set an alarm but doubted she'd sleep a wink.

CHAPTER FORTY-NINE

THE MARINA MARRIOTT HOTEL ENJOYED PRIME REAL ESTATE on the south side of the marina and looked out over the harbor. The sun was low in the sky, casting long shadows across the courtyard next to the restaurant patio.

Dawn stood with Megan, having said her goodbyes to the other students, and Gerry and Andy, following their interviews. The final interviews, with Megan and Timothy, had taken the longest. She yawned, the hours catching up with her.

"I'm sure that was exhausting for you," Megan said.

"It was long," she agreed, an understatement. The interview with Timothy had been wrought with conflict as he demanded information and details about the men. Information none of them had. In the end, everyone in the room had been frustrated with him. When he left, he'd made a big show of ignoring her.

"But you did great," she said. "I agree with everything they said in there. You really saved the day."

Megan blushed and waved her hand in the air. "No. You did."

"You saved Jenny."

"That I did do."

Dawn looked across the courtyard where Jenny sat having drinks under an umbrella with her super fans, Gerry and Andy. She'd draped a colorful scarf over her shoulder to hide her bandaged arm.

She looked fresher after the hospital. During the interview, she'd been composed and calm, sometimes animated, even bubbly at times. At Dawn's earlier request, they reminded Jenny, in stern terms, that she was not to share the details of the incident on social media. She pouted but agreed.

Dawn was relieved Jenny didn't seem to hold any hard feelings, but part of her felt like she was waiting for the other shoe to drop. That it was only a matter of time until somebody showed up with a lawyer or tried to sue her for damages. Jenny had the strongest case. It wouldn't surprise her a bit if any of them were approached by lawyers encouraging them to make a case. She needed to remember to get the signed copies of the Liability Waivers from Timothy.

Captain Birch and his men approached them. Younger than she'd previously thought, but still too old for her, she had to admit he was quite handsome in his dress uniform.

"Good job in there, ladies," he said, reaching out to shake both their hands again. Dawn had shaken so many hands during the course of the afternoon she was starting to feel like a politician.

"What happens next?" Megan asked.

"Next we'll compile all the interviews and—" The ringing of his cell phone cut him off. He dug it from his pocket and glanced at the number. "I need to take this," he said. "I've had it off for several hours."

The Captain stepped away and Dawn turned to respond to a question one of the officers asked her.

"It's for you," Captain Birch said, appearing beside her, and holding out his phone to her.

Surprised, Dawn took the phone and took a couple of steps out of earshot of the others.

"Dawn, Birch told me you saved the day out there last night. Or was it this morning? You know what I mean." Wayne Cutter chuckled. "I wanted to let you know that we've pulled out all the stops and we're going to find those two men."

"What does that mean, pulled out all the stops?" She fixed her eyes on a small speedboat cruising past the marina entrance.

"We have a couple of other agencies involved."

"Which agencies? Captain Birch didn't mention that." Why did things always get murkier instead of clearer? Since the fatal day she first met Wayne, she'd felt like she was deep diving without a light.

"He's not authorized to. And frankly, he's not privy to all of it either. Look, this is confidential, I don't need to tell you that. I just want you to be able to sleep at night knowing that we're on the job. We're going to get those guys."

Against all odds, Dawn wanted to believe him. She forced a brightness into her voice she didn't feel. "Thanks, Captain Cutter, I appreciate that."

"Wayne," he said. He paused a beat too long and she felt her chest tighten. If he spoke about Joe, or asked how she was doing, she wasn't sure she'd be able to keep it together. Her body thrummed with exhaustion, her emotions running much too close to the surface.

He cleared his throat. "I'll keep you informed."

"Thanks, Wayne."

She walked back to the small group and passed Captain Birch his phone.

"I was just telling Megan," he said, "that if either of you ever consider a change of career, the Coast Guard would be happy to have you. We have a training facility nearby, you know."

Dawn glanced at Megan, who grinned back at her. "I'm

pretty happy on the Papa Joe," Dawn said. "But I agree, Megan would be awesome at that."

"You know where to find me if you change your minds," he said. "I'd be happy to give either of you a personal recommendation."

They thanked him and stood shoulder to shoulder as he walked away with his entourage.

"Coast Guard, huh?" Dawn turned to Megan. "Think you'd do something like that? What do you do, by the way?"

Megan laughed. "I'm a financial analyst."

Dawn chuckled. "Well, it would be a change. In any case, you know your way around boats. We should stay in touch," she said, the words out of her mouth before she could corral them back.

Megan brightened. "I'd like that. Maybe we can do lunch."

"I'm not really the type to do lunch," Dawn said, heading toward the parking lot.

"Then invite me out on the boat one day. We can go fishing, or swab decks, or whatever it is you do all day when you're not fighting off bad guys."

Laughing, Dawn pulled out her phone and they exchanged numbers. "I'll call you," she said.

This time she was ready when Megan leaned in for a hug. It felt good and she realized she'd been holding herself away from human contact for far too long.

It was time to rejoin the world of the living.

That's something Joe would have wanted, too.

CHAPTER FIFTY

Late Saturday morning, Dawn lounged below deck, watching cartoons, drinking coffee and snacking on potato chips. Thanks to the failed course, the galley was crammed with groceries. Good thing, because without them she'd be hungry as well as broke.

When she made her coffee earlier, she considered packing some of the food up and taking it over to Timothy, but then, on her way down the dock to put a laundry in, he'd flipped her the bird on her way past. So much for that idea.

She put the chips down. Eating them wouldn't solve anything and she should get up and cook some bacon and eggs, or make a sandwich. There was some nice ham and cheese in the fridge.

Beside her, her cell chirped. She glanced at the notification on the screen. A text from Duncan.

Hearing went well. I'll be in touch later regarding your deposition.

That was cryptic. But no news was probably good news, as Joe used to say. She tossed the phone on the bunk and turned up the volume on the cartoons.

On the screen, Wile E. Coyote slammed into the side of the

cliff, his face plastered against the fake opening the roadrunner had painted on the rock. Eyes rolling in his head, body flattened, he slid down and crumpled into the ground like an accordion.

There. The epitome of her life lately. She barked out a bitter laugh. Despite her efforts, she was no further ahead than she'd been a few days ago.

Well, slightly ahead. Her dock fees had been paid by Duncan, so at least she had a place to lay her head for the next month. The groceries from the course would feed her for a few days. She'd freeze what she could and be sure to eat the perishables first.

After they refunded the students, she'd still have a huge fuel bill with the marina and she was determined to keep her promise to Timothy to reimburse his expenses. Only fair, since she was eating most of the groceries. He'd also paid for the alcohol and she wanted to get the small amount that Miguel and Jose hadn't drunk off her boat as soon as possible. She'd put the bottles in a box and dump it off at his boat.

No time like the present. With new purpose, she sprang off the bunk, gathered up the bottles in the galley and stepped outside to grab an empty carton from under the aft deck.

When she lifted her head, she spotted a small man in a dark blue suit—much too warm for a day like today—hustling down the dock with none other than Mrs. Howe at his side. He didn't need a sign on his forehead for Dawn to pin him as a lawyer.

She huffed out a breath like she'd been socked in the gut. Shit was hitting the fan faster than she thought it would. She really needed to make peace with Timothy and get those liability release forms.

"Oh, Dawn." Mrs. Howe's voice rang out, her hand flapping in the air like a small bird as they came closer, her cheeks rosy as apples. Her outfit was white and lacy with more ruffles than

Scarlett O'Hara's ball gowns. She looked like she was expected at a civil war reenactment later in the day.

Not wanting to have to invite them aboard—or have Timothy overhear her final defeat—she stepped down onto the pier and greeted them.

"This is the woman I've been telling you about," Mrs. Howe said to the lawyer.

"It's nice to meet you, Ms. Devon." The man stood stock still, his arms pinned to his side like a cut out. "Mrs. Howe asked me to come along and speak with you today."

"Okay." Once again, with lawyers, Dawn kept her mouth shut and waited for more information. Then she blurted out, "I don't have anything, Mrs. Howe. You can sue me but the only thing I have is this boat. If you want it, take it now and save us both the trouble of a lawsuit."

Mrs. Howe's lashes fluttered. "Oh my, Dawn, I'm not here to sue you."

"You're not?" She felt the heat creep up her cheeks.

"Chance, tell her." She prodded her elbow into the man's ribs. He was barely taller than she was.

"We're not here to sue you, Ms. Devon. In fact, we're here to help."

"I don't understand."

He reached his hand inside his suit jacket and pulled out an envelope. "Mrs. Howe wants you to have this. It's a financial contribution."

She shook her head. "I can't accept that. We're refunding all the money from the course." She looked at Mrs. Howe. "We already talked about this."

"Now Dawn," Mrs. Howe said. "I know you think I'm a silly old woman, but don't make the mistake of underestimating me. I know a lot more about the world than you might give me credit for." She winked and Dawn couldn't help but smile back at her.

"Here's the thing," she said. "As unfortunate as that whole incident was—and I feel deeply for Jenny, I do—it was also one of the best adventures of my life."

Dawn blinked as she looked into Mrs. Howe's sparkling eyes. The woman chuckled. "Also, it's given my husband a new story to tell at dinner parties. You can't imagine how tired I am of his stories, dear."

"Still," Dawn said. "I put your lives in danger, I can't accept payment for that."

"It's not payment dear, it's a gift. Consider me a ... patron, of sorts." She lowered her voice and turned away from her lawyer. "My husband has also become, let's say, playful again." She twittered and glanced back over her shoulder to be sure Chance hadn't heard her.

Dawn laughed and something inside her gave way, a release that felt really good.

Mrs. Howe placed her hand on her wrist. "Please take it, Dawn. I have more money than God. More than even Mr. Howe knows about." She giggled again, her voice that of a young girl. "I promise you I won't miss it and it will mean the world to me for you to accept it"

Chance stepped between them then—the man had excellent timing, she'd give him that—and extended the envelope to Dawn. "No strings attached," he said.

She met Mrs. Howe's gaze again. "No strings attached," the woman confirmed.

Chance placed the envelope into her palm, Mrs. Howe leaned in and kissed her cheek and thanked her, then they were gone, in a flurry of flapping skirts and tapping footsteps, back down the dock as Dawn stood watching them go.

And with that, it was done. No doubt the money would cover Timothy's debt and her own for many months. She could stay here forever, if she wanted, enjoying a life of ease.

But she couldn't. As long as the men who attacked her were

out there, as long as the men who killed Joe were free, she couldn't rest.

And she wasn't about to trust the system any longer. The system was too slow. The system was flawed.

If this trip had taught her anything, it was that it was time to bend fate to her will.

Time to rain down hell and beyond on the men who had wronged her.

It was time to fight back.

———

ABOUT THE AUTHOR

Riley Curts writes thrillers and action adventure stories, most set on or near the ocean in tropical settings.

At two years old, Riley was thrown into the river to learn to swim and is still here to tell the tale. A happy day is one spent in the water, preferably above the surface.

———

Don't miss Dawn's next adventure in GRAY DAWN as she takes to the seas when one of her new friends is kidnapped. Available now.

Visit the author's website at www.RileyCurts.com for upcoming release dates and other news.

Join the discussion on Facebook at fb.me/RileyCurts for insider news, previews, and cover reveals.

Find Riley at Goodreads.com/rileycurts

ALSO BY RILEY CURTS

TROPICAL COAST THRILLER SERIES

NEW DAWN - Dawn Devon - Book 1

GRAY DAWN - Dawn Devon - Book 2

DARK DAWN - Dawn Devon - Book 3
(Available 2022)